I'm thankful to God because without Him I would not have done this. I hope that this benefits and advises you the way that I intended it to. I pray that you all heal soon. I want to thank those who have constantly supported me through this journey; although this will never be able to show my gratitude, I appreciate everything that you have done for me.

Komal, Imran, Faisal, Shammas, Ali

For you guys who believed I could do this and gave me nothing but love and support - forever grateful.

Chapter One

There it was in her letter box; the white envelope that she had been dreading to receive. "Maybe if I don't open it, it will all just be a figment of my imagination. No I have to do this, it's time." She whispered to herself. She slowly opened the envelope, the paper rustling in tune to her pacing heart. Inside was a white card with gold coloured patterns.

"I don't think that I can open this," she mumbled. Her hands were trembling as she went to open the card. She froze, everything around her stood still. Even when she knew what was inside, the deluded part of her mind tried to believe that it was not true. Her fingers touched the card as she carefully removed it from the envelope. There it was in beautiful, calligraphic writing; his name right next to another woman's.

She stared at the RSVP on the invitation, moving her fingers over the names. She couldn't go, right? But then people would talk; they'd call her weak, or say that she wasn't happy enough for him. Little did they know how much she prayed for him to be happy, for him to find someone who was right for him. Even though someone else was living the dream that they would always talk about, she knew that his future did not involve her and that it was written this way. That was the thing about the way that she was brought up, she believed that putting your parents before the ones you love; out of respect and happiness, was the way forward. Arranged marriages were common for south Asians, but love marriages were becoming a lot more accepted compared to her parents day and age. Most of those arranged marriages were not forced marriages, but one at the choice of the parents, who introduce the son or daughter and then let them have the final decision. Many of her friends and relatives had successful arranged marriages which gave her a reason to never be against it, however she just thought that she would give love a chance and if that did not work out she would leave it to her parents.

She picked up the phone and held her finger towards the number she should have deleted, but never had the strength to. Inside she knew the number was never the problem; it was deleting the messages, the pictures, the mug shots from those late night FaceTime calls.
"He won't even recognise my voice; should I really call him?" She mumbled to herself. It was too late, the sound of the phone ringing suddenly shot to her ears. A few seconds later, she heard a voice answer the number that she never thought she would call again.
"Hello, who's this?" answered a feminine voice. She pushed the red button as fast as she could, her heart beating at the speed of light.

"What have I just done? Is she going to call back, or should I call again?" She debated to herself. As soon as she had calmed down her phone rang.

"Please be mum." She whispered as she squinted to see who it was. The words 'No Caller ID' flashed up and down across her mobile screen.

"H..h-hello?" She said nervously; and after what seemed like a very long and silent pause, a voice replied.

"Hello, you just called on this number." She knew in her heart who had just called her back but was praying that it was someone else. She wondered if they were sitting together listening to her on the speaker as she spoke, or did she just have his phone whilst he had popped out. He was never good at remembering to take his phone or his wallet with him, he was always ever so forgetful, leaving it on the train once a month at least.

"This is Inayah." Silence, *again*. Did she recognise the name? Did he tell her about their past? Perhaps she knew because he never deleted her number and saw it appear on Caller ID and that's why she called back. She was contemplating many questions and wanted to know the answers immediately.

"My name is Aleena. I'm glad that you called actually because I was hoping that we could meet."

"Why would we need to meet?" Inayah replied bluntly.

"I have some things to discuss with you about my fiancé."

"What about your...fiancé." Inayah asked, the word felt bitter on her mouth.

"It's really important and I think it's better discussed in person. So what do you say?"

"I guess. Yeah okay where should we meet?" She asked cautiously.

"Well I don't live too far from you but I don't mind meeting half way?"

Inayah wondered how Aleena knew where she lived when she had not mentioned it and assumed Yaseen had pointed out that detail as well.

"I'm sure you must be familiar with this café on Oxford Drive, opposite..."

"Barney's?" Inayah asked hesitantly.

"I'm guessing he took you there already then." Aleena replied. Inayah was decisive about whether she should reply to that question or not, but Aleena understood what her silence meant.

"Well I guess it seems like the best option as Yaseen will be working out of town tomorrow so we can meet then. Does that sound okay?"

"It sounds great." Inayah told her.

"See you tomorrow, goodbye."

The phone shut quickly as if someone had just walked in. Perhaps she took Inayah's number from Yaseen's phone after seeing it on the Caller ID, which would explain why she called back on a private number. Inayah was confused about everything that was going on and wondered whether she was just overthinking or not.

"Did I really just agree to this?" Inayah whispered.

6 months earlier

"So, blue or red?"

"Hmm blue, to bring out the colour of your eyes," he laughed.

"Stop being cheesy and my eyes are brown! Come on, just picture it, us walking together into the hall, me wearing a blue dress and you in your blue suit." She said whilst smiling at him.

"Yeah and me with another girl." He said with a cheeky grin. She opened her mouth in awe.

"Stop it! That's not a funny joke, at all!" She looked at him with the angry face that he could never resist. He got up from his seat brushing the creases out of his trousers.

"What makes you think that I'm joking?"

She hit his arm, hoping that he'd laugh but his smile started to fade.

"Look, whatever happens will happen, whether we're written together or not, we'll be strong," she told him reassuringly.

"I don't think that I can be strong. I don't think that I can imagine a life without you." He then noticed her eyes start to

fill up with the tears she'd always fight back in front of him. He shook his head and smiled.

"Would you come to my wedding though?" He asked, raising his eyebrows. Her mouth dropped again, but she laughed a second later, not realising how that exact question would haunt her months later.

Chapter Two

"Okay, Inayah you are crazy, why are you doing this? Okay now I'm talking to myself. Definitely crazy." She said as she stirred her coffee whilst she waited for the mysterious woman. Coffee; the smell was sickening but she learnt to grow to love the taste when it helped her stay awake in those 9am lectures. Questions pondered her mind as she sipped her coffee realising it had turned cold whilst waiting; she gulped it down with disgust. She looked around the empty café, hoping that Aleena would walk in soon. The door pushed open and the lively jingle of the bell made a sound. A woman stepped inside, her short heels clopping as she walked.

"Aleena?" Inayah said. The woman sat down not making a sound.

"Yes, I'm Aleena" There was silence, all that could be heard was the clinking of coffee cups. "I need to speak about you about Yaseen."

The name she once used to call every day, the one she used to put next to hers; the one she tried to erase. It had been a while since anybody had mentioned his name in front of her as if they were treading on landmines if they were to even utter a word about him.

"What about Yaseen?" Inayah cleared her throat. "He's your fiancé right? I received the wedding invitation…" she tried to change the subject.

"I know about your past with him, in fact it's not even in the past, it's the present right?" Aleena said with certainty. Inayah looked up puzzled.

"What?"

"You still love him don't you?" Aleena asked.

She tried to get words out of her mouth but silence took over. It was not easy to express, especially to the woman who most likely felt the same way about him.

"I admit that I used too but things with Yaseen ended and he's no longer a part of my life" Inayah said looking at the love of her life's fiancée. She was beautiful, her skin blushed in all the right places, she was petite and her hair was covered in a beautiful hijab.

"The truth is Inayah, I didn't want to tell you, but I'm the one who invited you to the wedding, not Yaseen. I'd really like it if you came." Inayah looked shocked, and after a moment of silence, finally asked.

"But, why?" She zoned out as if it had triggered a memory she did not want to bring up.

"Stop being so dramatic!"

"Yaseen, why do you always do this, why do you start these arguments?"

"You're always blaming me Inayah, we're both at fault"
"No, you do this to push me away, but Yaseen I'm just going to keep fighting for you" Inayah shouted as she walked away.

Day by day they'd argue, over the smallest things, it would break them and push them further apart.

"Inayah?" Aleena asked noticing Inayah had blanked out from a day dream. "I want you there to show Yaseen that you're strong enough to watch the love of your life marry another. So it will show him that you no longer care and that you are truly over him just like you told me you were. You understand right? I know it's a lot to ask but will you do it?" Aleena said. Inayah sat across her, her face was astonished, as if it was an evil joke.

"I don't think you understand what you're asking me to do. How can I come to the wedding? It's all in the past so why would I need to prove anything?" Inayah asked.

"Because before we accepted this relationship we discussed our past and he told me about you. The way he spoke about you, there was such passion in his eyes. I knew you'd always be in his heart. It scared me because I thought that he was marrying me to get over you, or worse; whilst he was still in love with you. I accepted because I thought that we could have a great future and I was guilty of falling in love with him, but I don't want to get hurt and more importantly I want Yaseen to be happy." Aleena replied.

Inayah sat silently, she never thought about how Aleena would feel about all of this and how much she'd start to care and love Yaseen. Of course she would, he could make anyone fall for him, one glance from him and it was as if the world had stopped and it was just the two of them. His smirk, his eyes, just the way he'd make you feel at ease just being around you.

"Me and Yaseen were like best friends with very strong feelings. That's all it was; there was a lot of complications. Our relationship? I don't even know what it was. We just grew side by side, getting to know each other and feelings got in the way. We couldn't sacrifice everything for a bit of happiness, it wouldn't have worked." Inayah replied. Aleena looked down, she had the look of an innocent child.

"Can you just think about it?" She replied.

"Aleena, you're asking me to do something huge. I can't face Yaseen, I really can't. I've prayed for both of your happiness before you even existed. It's a chapter that I have closed and me turning up to the wedding? I just can't." Inayah continued. Aleena cleared her throat.

"I understand and I'm sorry for asking you to do this, it's just that I was scared about starting a new life with Yaseen, I mean what if it doesn't end well?" She looked down again, a tremble in her voice. Inayah put her hand on her shoulder.

"Look, I know it's hard for you as well, but you wouldn't be getting married to him if he didn't want to start a new life with you. You're the right one, it was written this way, how many arranged marriages turn out to be fine?" She smiled.

'How can I be here advising the woman I never wanted to meet, like this?' she thought. The phone started to buzz. Both women checked their pockets.

"It's mine." Aleena said. "I have to go. Inayah don't tell anyone about this, especially not Yaseen, we'll talk soon." What more did they have to talk about? Inayah thought as Aleena left and waved goodbye.

Inayah sat thinking about what had just happened. Her head felt heavy as if the questions and thoughts on her mind were scratching at her.

"Inayah! I haven't seen you here for ages! Where's Yaseen?" A voice asked.

She turned around to face the man in the apron who was refilling the juices.

"Ted! Nice to see you, I guess you didn't hear about me and Yaseen, it ended." She said with a nervous smile.

"What? No! Are you serious? You guys were here all the time giving all of us a bit of hope that happy relationships exist." He laughed. "Unlike me and the Mrs who's well, you know." He sighed and laughed again. "But it's great seeing you, take care okay darling, you're always welcome here." He smiled.

"Thank you Ted, give Annie my love." Inayah said smiling. She made her way to the door and decided to walk home to take in a bit of sunlight.

"This tastes so good I swear, try some Inayah."

"Wow, that's amazing."

"Can we get married here?" He laughed.

"There won't be a wedding if we don't pass these exams, come on carry on revising I need to finish this essay too."

"I really don't want to. I'm so tired I need a break."

"Yaseen you've read one paragraph! Come on just read and take a bite after every paragraph to reward yourself."

"I think we should make this our spot you know, we've been here during the times we revised, the times we had our fights, and of course when we were just peckish."

"I think it already is." She laughed.

"Promise me that whatever happens between us, whether we're married with grandkids or not, if this place still exists

we'll come back in forty years and sit in this spot and look back at the life we lived and the moments that we made."
"Deal, if I remember you, I might forget you in the next year you know." She laughed.
"Hey! Now come on let me revise you're such a distraction." He grinned.

Chapter Three

Inayah struggled in deciding what to do and knew she had to make a decision that came from her heart. It was hard going through what she did with Yaseen because she felt judged and couldn't talk to people about it. She believed that a private life was a better life and all that she cared about was his happiness.

"Imagine if I was in Aleena's position...actually no why doesn't she imagine she was in mine?" She debated with herself, frustrated again at her dilemma. "But seeing Yaseen, in his suit, his hair not messy for once." She smiled and then stopped. She'd be watching her dream being lived by another, even though it had been destroyed in the moment that it had all ended and was now a nightmare. How could she stand in front of the one she loved all over again? The one she had to walk away from in order to save herself. He wanted to remain friends but he was asking for her to do something that she could not put herself through.

"You can't just walk away from me like this. I need you to be there for me through this Inayah, I need you in my life."
"It's all about you isn't it? Can you just imagine how much I'm hurting right now? I wish you the best Yaseen but I can't watch you with someone else I really can't pretend to be

happy for you."

"Inayah you have to understand I have no choice."

"I respect that, so give me the decency of respecting the fact that I will walk away right now and I do not want you to contact me, nor will I contact you. Goodbye Yaseen."

It had been a few days since she had met Aleena, and she still hadn't decided what to do. Aleena had not contacted her either which made her wonder whether Yaseen had found out about the situation and their meeting. She looked at the time and realised she was getting late for work so hurried into her car. It was a slow day at the office but at least she could stay occupied hiding at her receptionist desk and catching up on work that she was behind on.

Knock knock knock

She did not want to look up because only one person would knock on her desk at work this way.

"Yaseen." She exclaimed. She was silenced at the shock of him being in front of her again, flashbacks of their last meeting was running through her mind. He still had that messy stubble because he was always too impatient to grow a beard.

"Inayah when's your break? We need to speak urgently."

"Yaseen, you have to go; you cannot be speaking to me. Alee-"

"Aleena knows that I'm here." He interrupted.

"What do you mean? This whole thing has been a cruel joke hasn't it? You've probably been laughing at me this whole time together. Here's me feeling sorry for her and actually caring for the one who's trying to love you like I did, but no." She stopped as he looked up at her and into her eyes. She hated when he would do that as it always made her feel too weak to argue with him.

"No Inayah, it's not like that, she told me this morning and I came straight here. I wanted to check up on you and see if you were okay."
"Why are you really here Yas?" She questioned, seeing right through him.
"Truthfully, I need you to accept all of this so that I can too. Can we just speak about this?" He sighed.

They sat at the table, opposite each other after what felt like years. Yaseen shook his leg and tapped his feet on the floor. "You do that when you're nervous." Inayah said. He stopped as he looked up at the woman he thought he would never face again.
"Okay let's talk about this, about us."
"What us?" she interrupted. "There's no us Yaseen, we stopped being an 'us' a very long time ago, heck I'm struggling to wonder whether there ever was an us." He put his head into his arms, confused as to what to do.

"Inayah" He groaned, looking up once again. "I want you at the wedding, I need your support, you still mean a lot to me. I know it's not easy for yo-"

"Easy?" she scoffed, "You're asking me to do the impossible. I'll come into the hall, see the same colour setting we picked, see the decorations, the cake, your hand in hers." She shook her head.

"If I was in your position I would come." He mumbled.

"But that's the thing, you're not in my position and honestly I pray that you never are because it hurts, it really hurts Yaseen. When they ask me if I'm okay I tell them that I'm fine. I tell them that I'm concentrating on myself, focussing on rebuilding the life that you tore apart."

"Don't act like we didn't end it together. You're making me out to be a monster. You know I gave you all the love that I could, if we couldn't have a future that's not my fault, it was written this way. You said that you had accepted it and you clearly haven't. I'm sorry I picked my parents wishes before yours. I know that you're upset because you didn't think this would all happen so quickly but you're forgetting that you walked away from me too. I get it, we argued, we fought, we could have made it work but deep down we knew my life decision had already been made for me." He shouted, his eyes focused heavily on hers. He was breathing in and out, the temper clearly showing in his face.

"Yaseen." She could feel herself choking back on her tears, the feeling of guilt surrounding her knowing he was right and that her emotions were making her speak badly of him.

"I guess that this was a mistake and I tried, I really did. Do whatever you want Inayah, I wish you all the best." He made his way outside as she once again watched him stroll away, not a care in the world. How many times had they watched each other leave without holding on to their hands, pulling them back towards each-other?

"No don't speak to me, I'm not forgiving you for this."

"I'm sorry."

"No, you took it too far."

"I said I'm sorry." She pouted.

"Don't do that."

"Do what?"

"That face that makes me forgive you when you mess up."

"I love you." She pouted again.

"Inayah!" He laughed. "Stop it. One day that's no longer going to work okay?"

"Really?" She questioned, making the same face.

"Okay fine I forgive you." He said, shaking his head as he hugged her.

Chapter Four

Inayah sat thinking about the events that unfolded the day before. It was a hard choice but she had finally decided what she was going to do. She picked up the phone and finally dialled in the contact number on the invitation. A familiar voice answered.

"Hey, Inayah." Aleena answered.

"Hey, I've made a decision."

"Okay, is it a yes or a no?"

"I'm sorry Aleena, I can't do it, I wish you guys the best, but I will not be attending this wedding." It went silent and she heard a sigh.

"I understand, I was stupid for even going behind Yaseen's back and meeting you."

Inayah's heart started to pound as she wondered whether she knew about Yaseen coming yesterday and whether he lied to them both.

"Aleena, I need to talk to you about why I came to this decision."

"Inayah, I'll call you later someone's here I'm sorry, goodbye!"

Inayah felt as if she had been slapped across the face. She was confused, hurt and struggling a lot. This woman who she'd never wanted to meet or never wanted to care about; was marrying the love of her life. The man who showed her the meaning of love and also the meaning of heartbreak. But now she felt remorse for this innocent woman who just wanted to have a future with him; who tried to fix things and make it right before their fresh start. For her sake and their families' sake she wondered if she should try to help. It was nothing but a maze of complications and Inayah felt she had a duty to fix it. Who would have thought she would ever do such a thing? She knew deep down that she shouldn't have gotten involved in the first place, she had told Aleena the decision and that was it. There wasn't going to be a friendship out of this, she wasn't going to turn up at the engagement party with balloons and presents, making toasts to their loved ones. They were starting a new chapter and she should too. She had to concentrate on herself, her career and someday finding herself a companion too, whether it be arranged or love. *Love.* She wouldn't dare try to fall in love again; this is why parents knew best. This is why their religion and culture stopped them from being with others before marriage, it would definitely save them from the heartbreak. She sighed. She was always the one to advise others, but it seemed she fell for the same game that she despised.

Inayah made her way towards her laptop and sat down. Once more she refreshed her email box, constantly praying she would get a reply. *CLICK.* Nothing, not one new email. She sighed then closed her laptop. She needed a bit of good news after the week that she had experienced. She tried to take her mind off things and carried on applying for different jobs as she needed a change and wanted a job that was in the same sector as her photography degree. *'Another rejection...'* She thought.

"Inayah are you home?" Her mother called as she walked into the door.
"Yes mum." She called back making her way towards her mother. She greeted her with a kiss on the cheek and slumped down onto the sofa.
"You've been refreshing that mailbox again haven't you?"
"Mum you don't get it, I need this."
"And just as I have said many times you'll get what you want if it is written for you, only God knows what's best for you."
Inayah scoffed, then acted like she was coughing when her mother gave her a funny look.
'Don't I know it?' she thought. She just couldn't help but want the experience. She had been praying for it for a long time. But her mother was right, whatever was written for her was going to be the fate she'd receive.
'When one door closes, another door opens,' she thought.

She had a lot of responsibility as the only child; she had to work hard and help her parents all whilst she got an education.

She could never disrespect them and do something that they did not want her to do; after all, they always knew best and had always tried to protect her. She got into trouble at a young age when mixing with the wrong crowd even after her parents had warned her. After that she realised exactly why her parents did what they did and knew that she had to make it out there in the world alone and she wouldn't have her parents holding her hand forever. Therefore, she had to listen and always remember the things that they had taught her. Her parents never forced her to do anything that she did not want too, they supported the subject that she wanted to study at university and let her socialise and work in different places if she felt the need too. Inayah was very similar to Yaseen, they both had a lot of love and respect for their parents, which made it harder for them when Yaseen had to accept the choice that his parents had made. She always knew that her parents would have accepted Yaseen and been happy with the marriage. Yaseen's parents had fixed his arrangement with Aleena's family from a young age but as nobody had mentioned it for many years he thought that his parents could have come around to changing their mind as he grew up, but because of dignity and respect they did not.

"Izat." She whispered. The word flowing through her mind. It was a big thing in south Asian culture, *izat*. It meant respect, something many families put before anything. Most of the rules that were created, she sometimes felt were only followed by people because of *izat*. If someone wasn't dressed correctly or if someone was out late, it would ruin the families izat. It was changing as times became modern, but many families stayed very strict and she felt she was lucky that she still had some freedom.

As she sat wondering about Yaseen's family and remembering the struggles he had with his father growing up, she thought about Aleena and her family. Aleena seemed very quiet as if she would only speak out sometimes; but that was very judgmental, because Inayah seemed quiet at times, yet was usually called a loud mouth who would never stop talking. Aleena also wore the hijab and it made her face glow so delightfully. She walked over to the mirror and picked up her mother's scarf that was placed on the counter. She started to wrap it on her own silky hair and try out different styles, the way that the famous Muslim YouTubers would with their scarves. Her mother wore the hijab for numerous years but her family had never pressured her into it. At one stage of her life, she tried it too but she only lasted for a week. It was something that she had always wanted to try but felt that she could only do it fully when the time was right.

"I will one day, maybe after marriage."

"But Inayah, what if you die tomorrow?"

"Wow, that's so unfair Yaseen."

"No, I'm not pressuring you, the hijab is such a big step that's between you and God. I just feel as if we can never know what will happen next. Whether I go, whether you do, we can never know. We should live each day as if it is our last."

"That scares me. Imagining a life without you. Waking up and not hearing your voice, not feeling safe and protected. What if I can't tell you I love you one last time?"

"Inayah, I know you'll always love me. How can you not? Everyone loves me."

"You really ruin every moment don't you Yas." She laughed.

"But it's true, who couldn't love you."

Chapter Five

It was the day of the engagement party and Inayah still had not been able to tell Aleena about Yaseen coming to see her at work. She felt it was not her responsibility to do so. Once they were married it was a clean slate for them and she did not want to be involved. Their wedding would be soon and she did not want anything to change her mind about attending it.

It was a beautiful day the sun was shining but there was also a mellow breeze. She had to stay strong today, it was just the beginning of the test of her strength. However, her peace was interrupted by a heavy knock on the door. Upon opening the door, inside walked a suited and booted Yaseen. Her face looked astonished.

"No, not today please you cannot be here on your engagement day Yaseen. My parents are upstairs; they might hear you!" She screeched in a hush tone.

"I just need to know." He looked distraught as if he had spent the whole night lying awake.

"Need to know what?" She replied, confused.

"Would you have fought for me?" He whispered. She looked up at her best friend, her first love, her everything. He was asking her for a way back into her life, or an escape. She could easily tell him the truth, they could try again, he could finally have the confidence to tell his parents. They would understand right?

"What? Yaseen this isn't a romantic Bollywood movie where you stroll into the house in the last minute and realise that you're marrying the wrong girl. It does not work like that. Damn it you need to do this for Aleena and for your parents!"

"What about you? What about me?"

"Enough Yaseen, we were nothing, it was the past and it stays in the past. This is the way it was written. You can't let the past take control over the decisions of your future. I'll always love you but your happiness and Aleena's happiness, it depends on this. Just go."

"What if it was written for me to come back to you, to realise that we should have never parted. To show me that I cannot marry someone else when all I'm thinking about is the moments that we made."

"Yaseen, moments come and go, they are created every second. You're a mess and you're afraid, I understand that. The reality is you came here just to know one last time, to find someone to pull you out of all of this, but inside you know that you are making a mistake. You're being unreasonably selfish and if you really do or did ever love me then for my sake walk away Yaseen. Go to your engagement, smile in the photos, show your family that you are content and close this chapter for good."

With that she shut the door, sliding down and sitting against it. She did not want to send him off in the state he was in but for once she had to think about herself, just like he always did. The tears she had kept in throughout the whole week finally soared their way out.

'Selfish, careless, stupid, typical Yaseen,' she thought as she held on to her nose holding back the sniffles and steadying her breathing in case her parents were to hear.

"Why now?" She mumbled. Countless months she had spent trying to forget the memories they had made, wondering if it was all just a waste of time. She knew it was a test but had she not been through enough with Yaseen already? It was as if she had finally removed the knife wounding her chest and he had come back to push it back in making sure that nothing could heal. She did not need this especially not now when she was finally getting over him. Well at least that's what she told herself.

"Inayah are you okay?" Her father asked as he came down the stairs.

"Yes dad, how are you?" She said with a smile quickly wiping her tears before he saw.

"I'm just going to work, are you off today?"

"Yeah dad thankfully I am." She grinned.

"Lucky for some isn't it?" He said shaking his hand on her head ruining her hair. He made his way out of the house waving goodbye to her. She hardly saw her father because of his work timings, but sometimes he'd come home on his breaks and she'd be able to catch up with him. Her family and friends always said she was 'daddy's little girl' and his 'princess', but she was too stubborn to agree. Her relationship with her father was something that she would never break. even when she was to move away due to marriage; even the thought made her emotional thinking about leaving him. Inayah remembered the times when she was a child, when she would sneak downstairs at 5 am just to see him pray before work and she would join him so that he could be proud of her. She respected her parents a lot, it was something that she could not give up doing, even if someone put her in a position where she had to. She was thankful that Yaseen had the same respect towards his parents and the thought of him hurting them, made her think about how her parents would feel if she did the same, and she did not want to ever do that.

"Will your mother like me?"
"Yes Inayah, come on there they are."
"I'm so scared, no Yaseen, wait!"
"Mum, dad this is Inayah. Inayah, this is my mum and dad."
"Nice to finally meet you."
"You too dear. Finally meet the girl who makes our son actually do his work in school ey?" His mother said, giving him dagger looks. Inayah laughed.

"Come on guys let's go my teacher is waiting for us and Inayah needs to find her parents!"

"Good luck, hopefully he doesn't reveal too much." She whispered once Yaseen's parents had gone ahead.

"What, like how much I love you?"

"Get your cheesy...out of here. Imagine your parents hear you. Now go, you're making it so obvious. Bye, good luck." She whispered. He ran off after his parents and she looked up at the crazy, wild, yet most genuine guy in the world that she was completely in love with.

Chapter Six

Yaseen seemed to have understood the message, because for the last few days all Inayah could see on her Instagram explore page was 'Congratulations Yaseen and Aleena' photos. She sighed. She tried to stay strong; but realistically she spent most nights crying into her pillow. That poor pillow had felt her every tear and heard her every prayer. Her parents thought it was the stress of over-working, but she just wanted to keep away and keep her mind busy. She tried to get out but seeing her friends would only encourage them to ask what was wrong and truthfully they already knew.

Yaseen was confusing as he never knew what he wanted. He just wanted to be loved but he'd drop every opportunity because he was scared of commitment. He was so scared of losing people that he never tried to find them in the first place. He put on a front of acting as if they disliked him or that he did not care when deep down he was always hurting inside. She was the only one who understood and saw that. She wanted to fight for him. But instead she prayed for someone to stay by his side, to break his fears and love him the way that she did. The thought of that reminded her of their wedding and how there was only a short amount of time left. There was a little part of her that wanted to go, to give her a peace of

mind of moving on. Aleena suggested that it would help
Yaseen but perhaps it was the only way to help Inayah.
Deep down she knew that she would not feel confident enough
to go there with everyone watching her. Especially if they knew
the truth about her and Yaseen, she'd be the gossip of the
community. *Asians, always ready to talk to one another
about everyone but their own kids.* She knew that she had to
talk to somebody. It was never easy for her to get her feelings
across. She kept everything bottled in and felt saving others
was the only way she could help herself. Yet inside she knew it
would catch up to her and that one day she would break.

There was only thing that Inayah knew that she had to do, she
had to talk to her best friend about everything. She texted
Haya to meet up with her, even though she had not seen her in
a while. Haya was the one person who could either talk some
sense into her or make her realise what she truly wanted. She
was the exact copy of Inayah, they were even teased that their
names were pretty much the same, but their bond was similar
to sisters and she was forever grateful.
"I've done something stupid." Inayah told her, as they sat on
the swings; their favourite meet-up spot for a bit of ice-cream
and sunshine.
Haya looked at her sarcastically raising her eyebrows.
"What have you done *now?*" She laughed. But noticed the look
on her best friends face. "I'm kidding what's wrong Nay?"

"It's Yaseen." Haya stopped swinging. She looked straight at Inayah, opening her mouth. Inayah knew what was coming, a big lecture.

"Don't get annoyed but Haya I need your help, please you're all that I've got." Inayah explained the situation, from the invitation to the meet-ups, to the decision she had to make that was controlling her thoughts from day to night.

"Now that's hella deep Inayah, you've had a tough week, why didn't you tell me? Stop trying to go through these things alone."

"You know it's hard for me to open up to people, even you. I like to go through my struggles alone instead of bothering other people, everyone else has a million problems I don't need to pester them with mine too." Their smiles faded so quickly, there was a lot of compassionate glances towards one another, both perplexed as to what to do.

"Inayah you can't keep facing the world on your own, it's not easy for anyone to face things like you do. I'm here, so many people are here, no one will think badly of you if you come to us. Why can't you understand that?"

"I know." She sighed. She knew the truth deep down inside. It was the darkness of her mind that told her to stay quiet every time that she wanted to speak out. Her silent cries were actually cries for help, ones calling someone to tell her that it would all be okay. She had built herself up with an act of heartlessness, that nothing in the world affected her, but the reality was that she was just like everyone else. Alone, afraid and helpless.

As she waved goodbye to Haya she set off home. Haya was right about Inayah keeping things to herself and she knew that she had to share if anything else was to happen. Bottling things up was dangerous, but her stubborn mind got the best of her.

As she made her way past the flower shop she caught sight of a familiar face. *'No, not now. Please.'* She thought to herself.

"Inayah. It's been a while."

"Yes, it has. Congratulations on your engagement."

"Thank you. One step closer I guess." She looked down as if something was pondering her mind.

"Aleena, are you okay?"

As they took a seat in the local coffee shop, Aleena began to discuss her thoughts.

"You see Inayah, we've all been there. First crushes, first loves, first heartbreaks. But there is this fear that lives inside of me, one which keeps telling me that Yaseen will leave me. That he will go back to you and realise he had made a mistake with me. I can't live with this fear Inayah. It's haunting me. I sometimes wonder what would happen if he leaves me when I'm pregnant with our child, or even once the child learns to love his father, what if he leaves me then?" Aleena spoke softly, yet the distress in her voice was clear.

"Aleena, you cannot think like that. That isn't going to happen."

"But it has. It can happen again. Yaseen has the likes of my father. He is very similar. But do you know the last time I saw my father? I was ten years old, a younger sister by my side, an older brother left to look after my mother. He left us all alone so he could be with that other woman. He left it so late which made it worse because I remember every single memory we made; every birthday, every Eid, every talent-show and sports-day that he came to watch."

"I'm sorry that it happened to you but God knows best and Yaseen he wouldn't leave you like that."

"But he left you, so who is to say he will not leave me."

Inayah sat, struggling for words. Aleena's fears were eating her alive and she relied on the woman who had lived through them to somehow help her.

"Aleena you asked me what me and Yaseen were and I told you we were best friends whose hearts had gotten attached to one another. I loved him so much and yes he loved me. He loved me enough to leave me because he knew what he had promised his parents. How could he disobey them? Imagine he told them no, I will not accept the proposal, I will stay with the girl I love. What if they had never accepted and we spent our lives together never having the blessing from his parents? How could we live our lives that way? Your families grew up alongside one another, your parents had decided this from a young age, how could Yaseen break two families who were so close? There was so much about it that we would have sacrificed but the easier option was sacrificing ourselves Aleena. Yaseen, he has the biggest heart, he can learn to love so easily, he will love you, heck he probably already does. He would never hurt you, you have to have faith the way he has faith in his parents that you are the one who he should be marrying."

"Wow Inayah, you actually opened up to me about this situation, I really did not expect that."

Even Inayah herself was a bit taken aback by the words that had just left her mouth. Was it her way of accepting everything?

"Honestly, I wish the best for you guys. I better go. Aleena I never thought I'd say this, but I'll be here for you. Good luck." This time it was Inayah walking away, but for the first time in a while she was not confused, or upset, she did not walk away wondering if she had make the wrong decision. She was proud of herself, she knew that many people in her position could not do what she had just done.

"You have too much of a big heart you know that Inayah?"

"No, I just feel sorry for people and try to see the good in everyone."

"Even someone like me?"

"You? You are perfect the way that you are, I wouldn't change a thing. Well, I mean aside from you know."

"What?" He asked.

"That thing." She whispered.

"What thing Inayah?"

"Your marital status." She laughed.

"You are so cheesy did you really just use that line on me? I think my awful jokes are rubbing off on you" He laughed at her joke and pinched her cheeks when she frowned at him.

"If God wills, then one day. But for now, I'm spending every second I can to pray for that moment." He sighed.

Chapter Seven

"Where shall we go?" Yaseen asked whilst reversing the car from Aleena's driveway. They were going to get some dinner and go over a few more wedding discussions.

"The usual sounds fine."

"You're awfully quiet Aleena, you okay?" He had one hand on the steering wheel and propped the other on her shoulder. She shrugged it off lightly.

"I saw Inayah yesterday."

He was quiet for a moment, only the sound of the tyres hitting the potholes in the unsteady road could be heard.

"Did you plan a meet up? Or was it…"

"Coincidence…kismat I guess." She said, interrupting.

"Kismat. You really believe in that?" He scoffed.

"Yes, this same fate…this…kismat that brought you and I together."

"Okay…you met out of kismat. Then what? Why are you feeling so uneasy did she speak that negatively about me?" He rolled his eyes.

"Yaseen not one bad thing was uttered by her. I told her about some personal things, about my father and the fears I have of you leaving me."

He raised his eyebrows and shook his head, something he'd do when he was starting to get annoyed but knew that he had to remain calm.

"Aleena, I have told you so many times I will not leave your side. You are going to be my wife and we will start this new life together!"

"I thought you'd leave me like you left her."

He pulled the car up to the side of the road and turned the engine off. He started the tap his fingers against the steering wheel. Aleena opened her mouth to speak but was interrupted.

"Aleena, we're getting married in less than a month. We cannot go into this with negative thoughts. We cannot bring up the past of one another. I know you have been through these things and witnessed them but if you live your life fearing that these things will happen to you, then how will you ever learn from the lessons that you go through each day? Not everything happens to everyone. You are such an amazing person I could not do that to you."

"I know Yaseen and this is what Inayah was explaining to me, which is why I'm feeling this way, those fears, they are no longer at the back of my mind because she made me feel a lot less anxious than I was and I felt guilty for ever feeling that way. I'm sorry Yaseen. I'm sorry to you and to her. I just want us all to be okay with each other."

"Don't be sorry, look I get it and why you feel that way, I just want you to be able to talk to me and to realise that this is all going to be fine."

"Thank you Yaseen. I love you."

He looked over and gave her a reassuring smile, as he turned on the engine to drive to the restaurant, recalling thoughts of his past.

"I love you, I love you, I love you, say it Inayah."

"Urm, no, because I don't lie."

"Then why are you lying now?"

"Fine, I love you." She rolled her eyes.

"I love you too, see it wasn't that hard was it."

"It's easy for you, you're used to saying I love you to anyone, it's like saying hello for you." She laughed.

"Inayah, you're mad. 'I love you' comes out so easily for me to you because it's just another way to tell you how much you mean to me. It's only easy when I'm saying it to someone I actually love...duh."

Chapter Eight

'September 8th already,' Inayah thought as she opened her eyes and looked at her phone's lock screen. She pulled her duvet off and made her way to the bathroom. The reflection in the mirror stared back at her whilst she brushed her teeth, her eyes were puffy and her nose red from all the tissues to stop the sniffling. She took a deep breath as she heard her mother calling her.

"Yes mum?" She smiled as she walked in to the kitchen. Inayah knew inside she was a natural at smiling on the outside whilst constantly breaking on the inside, but she knew her mother also knew best and that she could not hide anything from her.

"Inayah, are you okay?"

"Of course, why wouldn't I be?" She asked, acting confused at her mother's question. Her mother gave a reassuring smile.

"There's a delivery for you. I left it in the dining room, maybe you should take it upstairs."

Inayah shot up, her stinging eyes making contact with her mothers. Both women knew exactly what the package was, but her mother stayed silent and left her to it. She made her way to the dining room and picked up the package and ran back up the stairs and into her bedroom. *Click*. She locked the door behind her and sat onto her unmade bed.

"You could never wrap these properly could you?" She whispered to herself, touching the roughly covered box. As she inhaled the overpowering scent, she ripped open the box. Inside was a bunch of tissue paper covering the contents inside, but she lifted up the white sheet of paper that lay flat on top.

Inayah,

By now you must have received something other than my usual yearly parcel and you have probably been contemplating whether you shall attend my wedding or not. I just want to say that I am sorry and I never had the chance to remind you about how sorry I was. I should not be explaining this all in a letter but I am hoping your kind heart will understand as you knew the invitation would be coming since the day I told you the news and we parted our ways. You see Inayah, a part of me still hoped that even after we left on bad terms you would still be there for me. The truth is every year we celebrate the day we first met, from the age of 11, and I send these parcels each year as a reminder because that was the moment my life changed. This is the first box I have sent since our relationship ended but I truly believe that it should not change the fact that we should cherish this day. I know you remember it so clearly, the first day of school, you came up to me with so much confidence, I was such a quiet, shy boy. (Oh how that changed didn't it?)

Remember how the first thing you said to me was, "You're short like me, maybe we can be friends!" and I laughed and agreed because you seemed just as crazy as me. Well look at us now, I'm double your height (Kidding, you're not that short...I think. Please laugh and shake your head and call me an idiot like you always do when I make short jokes.) But in all seriousness Inayah, regardless of whatever relationship that we had, that day you changed my life because I made a best friend and deep down inside you know that our friendship changed our life more than anything. Remember those days in class I would get in trouble and you'd get in trouble a second later just to join me in detention? Bad role model right? But like those moments, like the thousands of other moments, I need you to be there at my wedding. The most important day of my life, I need my best friend standing by my side. In the time that this letter and parcel gets to you, we may have come face to face and actually discussed whether you're coming or not, I do not know, I cannot predict the future. All I do know is that your heart is clear and I know you will do what is best for you. Happy meeting day, I hope that you enjoy this gift, maybe it will come in handy and I am sure you will look as beautiful as ever in it.

Yours Truly,
Yaseen.

Her heart was pacing, she was holding back the tears, yet smiling at every word as she thought about how much she really missed him. She put down the letter and removed the tissue paper from the box. She pulled out a garment which was covered in heavy embroidery. Her hands moved across the material as she felt each detail of the outfit. Each jewel was hand-stitched onto the garment, and was reflecting around the walls of her room. At that moment she could not hold back the tears and her smile had instantly faded. She clutched onto the divine clothes that he had given her and hugged it as it triggered a memory she had tried to push away.

"Look there!" She squealed as she pushed her nose against the window of the shop, steaming it up from her breath.

"Inayah," Yaseen laughed. "Get off there, come on try it on then."

"Are you crazy? I'm not even going to look at the price tag of this. It's designer! But wow, it's so beautiful. Yaseen, just look at it. Have you ever seen something so beautiful?" She squealed again.

"Yes, right now." He said, as she looked up to see him looking at the reflection of himself in the stores mirror. He laughed.

"Idiot." She laughed, then sighed and gazed at her dream outfit. "Someday right, I'll be rich enough to not even look at the price tag, to just go in and be like yep, I'll take ten of those." She grinned.

"Someday." He smiled.

Her emotions felt mixed each day, she was feeling indecisive and did not know what to do. She was pacing up and down the room.

"Maybe if I try it on." She said out loud, yet was shaking her head. She once more felt along the traditional Pakistani outfit, taking in how the colours intertwined so elegantly together.

Knock. Knock.

She unlocked the door and her mother walked inside.

"Inayah, I wanted to check if you were okay." She paused as she gazed over at the clothes. "Wow did Yaseen send that?"

"Yeah, for me to wear at his...wedding."

"Are you going?"

"I mean he invited me."

"I think that he would really want you there."

"Yeah I know mum."

"But take your time, you do not need to decide straight away I guess." She smiled as she left the room.

Inayah sat looking down on the floor, she knew that it was her decision and that her parents would always support her. They knew how close she was to Yaseen and everything they had been through. The days when she was in a bad mood the first question they would ask would be; 'did you have an argument with Yaseen?', which was usually true and would set her mood off even more. She was grateful that they never restricted the way her and Yaseen were and that they always saw him as a good, respecting man; something she always wanted her parents to see in her husband.

"Inayah aren't you ready yet? Come on go change, do your hair and make-up."
"I'm ready stop winding me up!" She stood still pulling an angry face at him.
"I'm joking." He laughed. "You look beautiful." He whispered.
"My parents will be here in a few minutes then we'll get them to take some photos of us okay?"
"Yes yes, that's fine. Inayah, I just wanted to say."
"Yes?"
"You look..."
"Yes?" She raised her eyebrows.
"Like you just woke up." He laughed.
"I hate you!" She screamed running towards him.

Chapter Nine

"How many times have you changed your mind by now?" Haya laughed.

"This is serious Haya, you didn't read the letter, it hurt me so bad."

"Do you not think that he wrote it to guilt trip you into coming Nay? See you're looking down because you know the truth you know what he's like. How many times has he emotionally manipulated you like this?"

"Stop it! Don't talk about him like that, I've told you not to do that so many times." Inayah could not take someone bad mouthing him especially when they did not know him the way that she did.

"But Inayah, how many times have I been there to pick up the pieces? You know that as your best friend I know you better than anyone and I know exactly what will happen. I'm only saying it to protect you, I don't even understand how you'll go there and watch him walking by her side, them smiling with one another, the way that you could have."

"Haya. I'm tired of defending this situation, I am so much stronger now. I'm pushing away the fact that we were together, that I loved him; he needs me as a friend, as a support system, who else does he have?"

"Who else does he have? Who else do you have? Where was he when he broke your heart and you turned to those temporary things that could take away the pain? I'm pretty sure he does not know about that. I was there, I saw it all and I cannot see you go through it again." She paused and lowered her voice as she noticed she was shouting.

"Haya I need my closure and maybe this is it. Yes, it will hurt but I'm moving onto new things, a fresh start. I'm doing this, and whether you want to be there for me if it all goes wrong, then be there, but if you don't then I understand. How many times have you not listened to me and you got so much out of it, whether it was a lesson or a blessing? Sometimes we need to make these choices and mistakes to learn from it all."

Haya groaned.

"How do you always get to change my mind so easily." She said as she hugged her best friend. "I'm sorry okay, I cannot ever put myself in your shoes and understand your thoughts, no wonder why you're always overthinking." She laughed.

If only things were as problematic as when they were younger, when their only worries were getting the latest toy in store before anyone else, or who's turn it was to ask their parents if they could stay at each other's houses. Growing up was something that they always wanted to do when they were younger; spending days playing 'grown-ups,' now they would do anything to have it that simple again.

"What are you going to wear, and how are you going to do your hair? Wait what about make-up? You cannot look too good because imagine that he sees you and stops the wedding and runs to you and-"

"Haya. Stop." She laughed and shook her head.

"Hopefully you can look good enough and one of the guys there comes over and Yaseen will see and get jealous, but you carry on talking to the guy and end up being soul mates and soon we'll be deciding what I'm wearing to yours and the guys wedding."

"Now who's overthinking?" Inayah said, laughing once more at the things Haya was coming out with. "But no, there will be no meeting another guy, how can I even look at another guy with Yaseen's whole family staring at me? Don't forget that some people knew about me, in fact most had even met me, they will either give me a sympathetic look or they'll be shocked that I even showed my face."

"But regardless, he will look over and stare at you, like wow Inayah." She mimicked Yaseen fainting when seeing Inayah, almost falling for real.

"Stop." She had laughed so much after days of tears and it felt good, she knew she made the right choice going to Haya; as crazy as she was, she knew how to save her when she needed it. But she also knew that Haya was right about him seeing her and wondered what he would think? She did not want anything to happen that could mess up the wedding. She did not know how she herself would react to seeing him? All those years of fake smiling and acting happy on the outside might pay off on those little moments, but she had to prepare herself enough to be ready to face everyone. There would still be a lot of people questioning the situation when she would get there, but she had faith that it would be okay; or at least she hoped that it would.

Inayah made her way home and knew that she needed some rest as the events of the past few weeks made her lack sleep because she was up all night thinking about things.
She finally got into bed and rested her head onto her pillow, imagining the wedding and how everyone would look. Her peace was interrupted by the buzzing of a phone call.
'Of course, as soon as I get to sleep my damn phone rings.'
She thought to herself.

"Hello." She picked up, her eyes half closed not looking at who had even called.
"Inayah, it's me Noor, Aleena's sister."
"Oh, hey. Is Aleena okay?" She asked, realising how concerned she must have sounded, after she had said it.
"Yeah, she's fine don't worry." She laughed. "Actually I called from her phone to ask you something."
"Sure, what's up?" Inayah said, trying to hide her yawn.

"Well you see…and I understand if you want to say no, it's just that I think, well, Aleena would be very happy if you came to her dholki tonight. I mean, I get that it may be awkward but I mean, you know?" She was not making any sense.

"I…urm, I don't think that's the best idea." She nervously laughed. "I really appreciate it, but you know."

"I completely understand Inayah, thank you anyways I just thought I'd ask anyway since Aleena said you're not sure about the wedding still and I thought maybe the dholki would be okay since Yas-, since the guys won't be there." She said. Inayah noticed how she stopped at Yaseen's name, not wanting to make it even more awkward than it already was.

"Thanks for asking anyways, actually Noor maybe you can tell Aleena, that I'm confirmed for the wedding actually."

"Really?" She said in a surprised tone. "I mean that's amazing, like you don't understand how much this will mean to my sister. I'll let her know, thank you so much Inayah, take care of yourself, bye!"

"Bye Noor."

Everyone seemed to act like it was such a big favour that Inayah was coming, she did not want them to think she was starting a fresh start with them being in her life, she wanted them to understand that she was only closing a chapter instead, as harsh as it sounded. She did not like going to dholkis', they were mini parties before the wedding where the ladies would sing, dance, play the drums and eat all sorts of food to celebrate the wedding. They could last up to a week, if there was one on every night and she felt that she was always tired from them, she would get home. Therefore, she felt that she did not need to go, if she was not going to enjoy herself, she did not want people to talk and say she was miserable because she was jealous.

Inayah knew what she really needed was the sleep that she attempted to have before the phone call and closed her eyes to get the rest that she deserved.

"I want a big wedding with loads of fast cars and we have to invite like the whole town and party all night."

"No way Yaseen, let's have a quiet one, I don't want all these people staring at me."

"Me either you're going to look so beautiful, imagine all those people that'll stare at you."

"Aww jealous are we?"

"Instead of me, damn it's not fair." He laughed.

"One day you'll be serious." She rolled her eyes.

"I'll change your mind don't you worry, you're the most indecisive person that I know."

"Hey! Okay that's true." She laughed agreeing.

Chapter Ten

It had been a long few days of overtime at her work as her co-worker had called in sick due to a stomach bug. Inayah perched herself onto the sofa, relaxing in her pyjamas even though it had not even hit 4pm yet. It was one of her joys in life to be able to relax in comfy clothes, watch movies and eat junk food.

Knock Knock.

She groaned and got up to open the door. She was never able to relax anymore, it was as if someone could sense her sitting down in peace, like when her mother would make her get up to bring something as soon as she had finally sat down.

"Yaseen. You're here again." She said opening the door. She thought about the first meeting since everything, where her heart was pacing just looking up at him, to the day of his engagement where she had to restrict herself from feeling anything by acting heartless.

"Hey, Inayah arc your parents in?"

"No, mum will be home soon and dads at work."

He followed her in and sat onto the sofa, looking around at the ice-cream on the table.

"Cravings?" He smiled.

"Yep." She answered quietly. "So why are you here?" She asked getting straight to the point.

"So, Aleena told me that you decided to come to our wedding...my wedding. Sorry."

"News travels fast." She said crossing her arms.

"What changed your mind?" He asked.

She thought about the letter and the parcel and whether she should tell him how it made her feel.

"I think it's the right thing to do for closure."

"Yeah. Well thank you it means a lot to me."

I'm not doing it for you. It's for myself.

"It's okay."

The keys jingled in the door and both Yaseen and Inayah looked towards it. Inayah's mother walked inside and looked back at the two of them.

"Yaseen, how are you dear? It's been a while."

"I'm okay, everything is good, how have you been yourself?"

"Yes very good, how's the wedding preparation going?"

"It's okay, I was just talking to Inayah about it. You're coming right?" He said turning to her mother.

"No, we aren't here I'm afraid. But Inayah will be there on our behalf." She smiled. "Would you like anything to eat whilst you're here?"

"No thank you, I have to go soon, I just wanted to talk to Inayah really." They said goodbye and her mother left them to continue their discussion in private.

"She always thought the world of you Yaseen."

"I know and she was always like a mother to me." He sighed.

"Remember those times when we were scared to talk to each other in front of her in case she would get angry." Inayah said laughing.

"Yeah until one day she saw us and I hid behind the tree and she laughed like oh so you're Yaseen." He replied. They both laughed until it went silent.

"At that age we don't realise how things will change as we grow." Inayah sighed.

"Yeah you're right. One minute we're playing in a tree house, or seeing how high we can swing, and the next minute everything jumps at you. You get responsibilities and you have to grow up so much quicker than you ever expected to. When I have kids I want to tell them not to be in a rush to grow up, to live life for a while you know?" He said. She smiled and nodded, but he knew her thoughts.

"Sorry, I didn't mean to bring that up."

"You're going to make a great husband and an amazing father Yaseen." She smiled again, reassuringly.

"I better go. I'll see you soon I guess." He did not wait for her reply and left the house urgently. Inayah looked out the window and watched him walk towards his car. A month ago she would not have been able to even say Yaseen's name without her heart aching and her tears flowing. She felt pleased with how much she had improved from the person she was to who she was today. Here she was facing the love of her life who she once imagined a wedding with, a family with, it was the hardest thing and she thought she was being very strong considering everything.

"No I don't like that name."
"You don't get a choice, I'm going through the pain of child birth, I think I should pick the name at least."
"Fine as long as we have my suggestion as the middle name."
"No, I don't like that."
"Fine. Whatever you say my queen, as long as they're a part of me and you, I will love them regardless. But let's hope they have your eyes." He said looking into hers.
"Hopefully they don't look like you because you know." She said going cross-eyed and sticking her tongue out.
"What was that?" He said, raising his eyebrows.
"Nothing." She said squealing as he started to tickle her.

She made her way into the kitchen to wash the dishes looking out into the garden remembering the memories they made there, from playing games to just laying on the grass looking up at the sky.

"Inayah are you okay?"

"Yes mum, I'm fine. Thanks by the way."

"For what darling?"

"Still giving Yaseen respect and love regardless of everything."

"Look these things happen Inayah. I was twenty-one years old, it happened to my best-friend, the one she wanted to marry she could not, her father would have never accepted him, she did not even try to argue. She married the choice of her father and yet here we are twenty or so years later and they are happily married with a grand-child on the way. Sometimes the sacrifice for your loved ones is not always a bad thing and I am so proud of the way you have been. I know it was hard, I wanted to be there for you but I know you like to deal with things on your own, you got that from your father."

"Mum." Inayah said, but couldn't look up her mother, who's eyes were starting to fill up.

"I love you darling and I really want everything to be okay, so I must ask you, I know you are going to the wedding and I know you are talking to Yaseen and being normal, but really deep down, are you okay?"

"I am okay and if I'm not one hundred percent okay, then I will be. I have faith and that's something that I can never let go of."

She smiled and hugged her mother, who loved and supported her so much. She was forever grateful she did not know how she would have coped without her mother.

"Things will get better you know that right Inayah?"

"I hope so."

"You just have to have faith because every day is another day and if you clutch onto the events of the day before how can you get forward?"

"I just feel like everything in my life never goes right."

"But this is what makes us into stronger people. If you had it easy, would you be grateful for when you achieve it and looked back and saw the steady road? But when you look back and see every single downfall and how you pushed yourself to keep going, now that itself is strength."

Chapter Eleven

'Hey it's Noor, hope you don't mind that I saved your number. Today we have another dholki, and it's going to be a main one as we're not doing an actual mehndi event but Aleena's going to get her henna done and we're putting haldi (turmeric if you don't know) on her face. I know you did not want to come but the truth is, Aleena hasn't got many people in her life and I meant it when I said she would really appreciate it, but once again I understand if you can't! Thanks, N xx'

"It's one thing after the other isn't it." Inayah thought as she went to look in her wardrobe for clothes.

'Dress code? – Inayah x'

'OMG. She'll be so happy I can't wait to surprise her. Wear yellow! Thanks once again, N xx'

Inayah pulled out an outfit and ironed it carefully, worried that she would burn it. She wasn't sure why she had agreed to come but she knew the whole series of events had her thoughts spinning round and round. Throughout the day she prepared herself by buying a gift for Aleena to present to her when she went to her house. She scoffed at the fact that she had changed her attitude towards turning up to celebrate with Aleena in a matter of just a few weeks.

Inayah then got ready for the dholki and wondered what everyone would be like and whether they would be as inviting as Aleena's sister.

Inayah took a deep breath and knocked on the door of Aleena's house. The door was slightly opened but she did not want to intrude and she could already hear the sound of drums, ladies who could not sing, as well as the sound of children playing in the background. Noor came to the door and dragged Inayah inside.

"I'm so glad you're here, wait till Aleena sees you, she'll be so happy!" Inayah gave a nervous laugh and followed her to one of the rooms.

"Inayah you came." Aleena said as she looked up from the floor where she was sitting.

"Yeah, wow you look so beautiful."

Aleena smiled and indicated with her eyes for Inayah to come and sit next to her. She did not have on her scarf, considering there was no outsider men there and her hair looked long and curly. Her outfit was yellow, and her sleeves were rolled up as she was having henna put onto her hands and arms. Aleena looked happy, her smile was not going away tonight.

Throughout the time of Inayah sitting next to Aleena, she must have been introduced to at least fifty different ladies, who she had forgotten the names of after seconds.

"Inayah this is my mum. Mum, this is my friend Inayah." Aleena said as her mother went to hug Inayah.

"Nice to finally meet you darling, would you like a drink or anything to eat?"

"No, I'm okay thank you very much." Inayah replied. Aleena's mother left to go join the ladies who were singing songs on the other side of the room.

"Find the initials." The lady putting the henna on Aleena's arm whispered to her.

"Initials?" Inayah asked, causing Aleena to laugh.

"Yes dear, initials. There is a well known tradition that when the bride is getting married and having henna put on her, we also put the initials of her husband-to-be, it's just a little game really." The lady said as Aleena blushed. "Can you see it?"

Inayah looked around the beautifully covered hands and arms of Aleena, searching widely for the 'Y' that could have been on her if Yaseen was still hers.

"I can't see it."

"I can." Aleena giggled, like a young teenager who had spent the day writing her initials next to her crushes in a heart.

"Never mind. As long as you can find it when it's your time." The lady said laughing and nodding to Inayah.

Inayah went silent, she did not like people mentioning her future, especially her marriage which was something she had not even thought about once since Yaseen. Aleena sensed that Inayah felt uncomfortable and told Noor to take her to go and get some food as she would get bored waiting around for the henna to finish.

They helped themselves to some tasty food, and Inayah complimented Aleena's mother who had cooked it all herself.

"Ladies, it's haldi time!" A lady shouted to bring everyone together.

One by one everyone started to line up next to Aleena and they each dipped their fingers or hands in the haldi, which was made of turmeric and other ingredients to create a soft orange and yellow mixture. Once it was on their hands they each placed a bit on Aleena's face, mostly with tears in their eyes. It seemed to be a very emotional moment and she could see Aleena trying very hard not to cry. At that moment it was Inayah's turn to put the haldi on Aleena. Aleena looked up and smiled. She was so humble and always grateful towards Inayah, even after everything. Inayah struggled to find a fault in her and knew inside she was happy that Yaseen was marrying an amazing woman like Aleena. She placed the haldi on her face and Aleena sniffed trying once more not to cry. At that moment Aleena pulled Inayah closer and dipped her own finger into the haldi trying carefully not to ruin her just dried henna. Inayah was not sure what was happening, but Aleena rubbed the haldi onto Inayah's cheeks and smiled.

"For you and your future." She said, this time a tear actually leaving her eyes. "I can't thank you enough."

Inayah was confused and twitched her nose. She could not control her emotions and let out many tears. She walked away sniffling, trying to wonder how she let this woman capture her heart so easily, she was like a sister that she never had, and she just wanted for her to be happy.

"Are you okay?" Noor asked Inayah.

"Yeah, are you? It must be hard for you too, losing your sister like this."

"It is sad, but she's so happy and she's starting such an amazing chapter of her life and I know Yaseen will treat her right." She said, suddenly pausing. "I'm sorry I didn't think."

"It's okay. I want them to be happy, that's what I've prayed for from the beginning." She said. "But I don't understand, why did Aleena put the haldi on me?"

"Oh these traditions honestly I don't really believe in them but it's said that when the the bride-to-be puts haldi on their unmarried siblings or friends, they will soon find a partner, and it's supposedly a good-looking one too!" She laughed. "I didn't let her put it on me I'm still too young to get married!" She said noticing Inayah's face start to look stern.

"Inayah don't be mad, look don't believe in this stuff! I know I don't, because honestly it's just silly traditions."

"I have to go. Thank you for everything, but I really have to...just go." Inayah said, her mind all over the place. She walked out of the house without saying goodbye to anyone. She ran into her car and drove home as quickly as she could, she just wanted to escape it all. Inayah did not understand why hearing the meaning behind what Aleena did had hurt her so much and wondered if it was the thought of her own marriage. "Why am I going in circles, I act like I'm okay when I'm really not, I am hurting. Are you Yaseen? Are you okay about all of this, or are you just putting on an act, because this feeling, these emotions, everything it just hurts." She cried taking deep breaths shouting at the reflection in the mirror, her make-up smudging over her face.

"I'm a mess." She sniffed taking more deep breaths.

"Why are you crying? What's happened?"

"It's nothing come on let's just go."

"No, I'm not moving until you tell me Inayah."

"Everything just got to me."

"This is why you shouldn't keep it all in I've told you, I'm here to listen."

"Yaseen, you have your own problems I can't suffocate you with mine."

"The only problem I have is knowing that you feel that you can't talk to me about these things when your happiness takes away any pain that I have, you know that right? Because knowing that you're not okay, honestly it makes me so upset Inayah. So let me wipe these tears and you go ahead and tell me what's wrong. I'm here okay, always."

Chapter Twelve

"Mum! Where are you? Guess what, guess what!" Inayah said running down the stairs.

"What's happened? Inayah you're scaring me!"

"I got an interview to be a photographer at 'over-clicking' in two hours! They said to come in as soon as possible! Mum, please pray that it goes well you don't understand how much I need this."

"Inayah, you know what I'm going to say to you, if it's written for you then you'll get it and if you do not then please don't be disheartened because-,"

"Yeah, yeah, better things I know." She replied, causing her mother to raise her eyebrows for mimicking her.

"Good luck my love, you'll do amazing." Her mother replied, kissing her cheek."

Inayah made her way to the interview and double checked the time.

"You got this Inayah, this is the fresh start that you need." She whispered hoping that no one who was interviewing her had just heard her talk to herself. All around her was people in smart clothing, with their heels or shoes clicking up and down the reception. She made her way to the front desk and cleared her throat.

"Uh…Hi, I'm Inayah, I'm here for my interview, I think I'm a bit early, sorry about that." She said nervously laughing.

"Inayah, yes nice to meet you I'm Becky." She said shaking her hand. "If you want to take a seat on the sofa there, someone will be with you in a few minutes. Would you like anything to drink whilst you wait?"

"No thank you." Inayah replied, smiling as she went to sit down.

She looked around the building and could see certificates on the walls for all sorts of awards, as well as paintings and photos of scenery.

"Hi, Inayah?" A gentleman asked as he went to greet her.

"Yes, hello that's me." She said shaking his hand in response.

"Nice to meet you Inayah, I'm Adeel. Right, if you want to follow me."

He made his way through the building and towards a small room; as she followed him through the door, they sat down on the chairs opposite one another with only a table between them. He offered her a drink but she kindly refused. Her new potential boss looked very young for his job role, as if he was only a few years older. He was a tall gentleman with a clean, groomed beard but messy hair. He was wearing grey trousers with a white shirt but the sleeves were rolled up. His eyes were brown but were hidden behind the glasses that he wore, she was looking at them to notice whether they were prescription or fashion glasses.

"They're just for fashion to be honest."

"Urm, sorry what?"

"The glasses, that's what you were thinking right?" He asked. She started to blush because she did not realise that he had noticed her staring.

"Urm, yeah you look good. I mean, they look good. As in, they suit you." She said, choking on her own words in embarrassment.

He laughed and she was somewhat relieved.

"I looked at your portfolio and I was really impressed." He smiled. "So let me ask you then, what is it about photography that you like?"

"Urm." She cleared her throat. "You see I just love capturing every moment that I can. I feel like people tell you stop and take the moment in, but the truth is why not stop and capture it? The second that you do, it is as if you can always re-live it, always look back at the photo and remember the feelings you felt, the views, the smells, the sounds. It's like a time-travelling machine back to the very moment when you clicked. Having the ability to do that and give someone that, is what I love about photography." She said passionately.

"I see." He said nodding, trying to hide his smile. He then proceeded to ask about her availability and tell her more information on the company.

"Part of the job means that you'll be travelling around, whether it be in this country or another, are you okay with that?"

"Yes, that's fine." She said, not actually sure whether it was fine or not.

"Okay, well Inayah, I'm pretty impressed with you, and I think I'd like you to start straight away." He said smiling.

"Really? Wow, thank you so much Sir it really means a lot. I won't let you down."

"Please call me Adeel. I know you won't. I'll contact you with further information as soon as possible. It was nice meeting you, I'll see you soon Inayah." She walked out smiling with joy hearing that he had given her the job. After the last month that she had experienced she really needed something to uplift her.

'See Inayah I knew that you could do it. Everything's been so hard I know, but this just shows that through every downfall, there is something positive waiting for you. Don't ever give up Inayah, you have so much to look forward to in life, so much that you can still achieve, now take this job as a beginning of your new chapter. Good luck my dear – Mum xx'

She smiled at the text that she had received from her mother, knowing that she was right. Although she had ups and downs recently, deep down she knew that there will always be greatness waiting for her, even if it meant being patient through the hardships.

Inayah took out her laptop and began to search up more about the company that she would be starting at. The first page had a bunch of photographs and customer reviews. She moved the arrow and clicked on the 'Meet the Team' section. She clicked on her new boss Adeel's profile and began to read.

'From a young age Adeel has began capturing moments that would forever be cherished in the hearts of whoever he would share them with. He worked his way through little jobs, training himself in skills to progress the best that he could. He studied photography at university and whilst getting his degree he started up his business at the age of 20. Now, at the age of 24 Adeel hopes to keep building and letting the company grow whilst training and working with other individuals in order for them to pursue similar dreams to his.

"Wow, he seems like a really amazing guy." Inayah said.
"Who does?"
"Dad! You scared me. Urm, no one! Well my new boss."
"Let me see. Wow very successful yes, he also looks really familiar actually."
"Really?"

"Yeah maybe he's local. Anyways Inayah, I said it already but congratulations, you really deserve this. I know how hard you worked to get yourself through university and to find the job that you wanted. All those hours at the reception may not have seemed worth it but it was all about patience wasn't it." He said, hugging his daughter.

"Thanks dad." She said smiling.

"Aww, look this one is actually nice."

"The person in the photo? Yes, I agree he is very handsome."
He said making her frown and shake her head. "I'm kidding. Wow Inayah, this actually came out really good. I'm impressed, you really have to pursue this you know."

"No, it's just a hobby, come on."

"No, Inayah, you have such a passion for photography, why not make it into a career? You've always wanted to go to university but didn't know what to study, well why not do something you're interested in and are actually good at?"

"I don't know Yas, what if I'm not good enough?"

"Inayah if we spent our whole lives wondering if we were good enough to do anything then where would we be? For a moment, forget everyone and imagine yourself behind the camera doing what you love. Does it matter about anyone else? No, because your happiness, your dreams and goals are more important than any of that. So what if you fail, you get back up and keep trying, how else will you get forward?"

Chapter Thirteen

"The colour has come out so dark, it looks amazing." Aleena said in awe at the henna on her hands.

"You know what that means right?" Her mother replied.

Aleena shook her head. "It means that your marriage will go very well, that your mother-in-law will love you more." She continued.

"Really?" Aleena smiled gazing at her hands once more.

"I don't believe in all that, I mean come on!" Noor shouted in the background. "It's an Indian tradition right?"

"Yes it is Noor, but it's just a bit of fun really, you can believe what you want too they will love you regardless." Her mother answered, kissing Aleena's cheek, trying not to tear up again.

"Just two days to go." Noor said, trying not to get everyone emotional.

"My daughter's going to leave my side." Her mother sighed. "I've watched you grow, I still remember the time you took your first steps, said your first word and went to nursery all alone." Her mother replied.

"Mum! You still have me you know?" Noor shouted, laughing.

"I know, but with any of you two, giving away a daughter is the hardest thing a mother and a father have to do. It does not matter about the distance or how caring the family is and how happy you know that they will be; it's like giving away your life." She said tearing up.

Aleena and Noor hugged their mother. It was going to be very emotional and they had to all stay strong during the process.

"Have you spoken to Yaseen? How is he feeling?" Aleena asked.

"He's coming over in a while to confirm the last few details, he's very stressed because he's dealing with a lot, but it will all be worth it and he knows that." Noor said.

"He's stressed? That doesn't make me feel better. He shouldn't stress." Aleena replied, starting to panic.

"Don't worry, it's a wedding these things are bound to happen."

Aleena sighed. A few days and it will all be over, she will be in a new house, with a new husband, a whole new life for the two of them.

A few hours later the doorbell rang and Aleena went to the door.

"Hello beautiful." Yaseen said walking inside. She blushed, looking down.

"Hi Yaseen. Come in, how are you feeling? Can I get you a drink or something to eat?"

"Urm, yeah just some orange juice will be fine." He said smiling at his bride-to-be. She gave him some juice and sat opposite him.

"How are you feeling? I heard that you're stressed."

"No not at all, it's just a few bits and bobs that I need to sort."

"Oh okay I'm glad."

"Yeah just making sure that everything is confirmed really." He said, sipping on his drink. "Your henna looks really nice and it's come out really dark too." He said, winking.

"You know about the meaning?" She blushed looking down.

"Yeah I remember ages ago, In-...someone told me." He cleared his throat.

"She came the other day to the dholki, it meant a lot to me." Aleena told him.

"Did she?" He asked. "That's good."

"Yeah, I'm not sure how she is now, she kind of left without saying bye, I'm not sure what happened."

"Oh, I see." He said. "I'm sure she'll be fine she gets over things pretty quickly."

"Like you?"

"What? I meant when she's mad." He said, raising his eyebrows.

"Maybe she just couldn't stay mad at you, do you not think?" She smirked.

"Aleena, can you just stop." He said shaking his head.

"I'm sorry, I'm just worried about her, I hate knowing my friends are upset."

"Aleena, if I'm honest, I don't think that you'll be gaining a friendship out of this you know. I mean, I know Inayah is probably doing this for our sake but I don't think she wants this to be long-term."

"You've spoken to her?" Aleena asked.

"No, I just know her well." He mumbled knowing he had lied.

"Are you a bit stressed about seeing her after so long?" She asked.

"Urm, no, I just said I'm not stressed, it's okay it will be fine."

"I know but it's been ages, when was the last time you saw her? After your relationship ended?"

"What's with all these questions? Let's just forget about Inayah, whether I see her or not, we'll be so busy during the wedding that we may not even be able to speak to our own family members let alone Inayah."

"I was just saying, there's no need to get so defensive about it." She said quietly.

"Look anyway I have a lot to do, so I better go. I'll see you on the wedding then I guess. Take care of yourself and give my love to the family. Bye Aleena." He said walking out of the door.

"Try not to stress too much." She said calling towards him with a smile on her face. She knew deep down that she may have hurt him, but the questions were on her mind and she wanted to go into the marriage with everything being cleared.

"Why aren't they up yet?"
"Yaseen calm down, they will be soon."
"I'm stressing out right now and it's making me angrier that they haven't released them yet!"
"Look you'll be fine you worked so hard honestly if anyone deserves to have passed it will be you. Do you remember when you once told me that if you don't do well, then don't be upset because it was for a reason and better things are going to come your way?"
"Yeah I know."
"So go on just calm down and have patience."
"Inayah, they're finally up. I don't want to check I can't do this."
"Yaseen, you got this. Take a deep breath and look."
"I PASSED. I did it!"
"I told you that you'd do it, I'm so proud of you."
"Thank you, sorry for the overload of stressing and shouting at you."
"It's okay, I know you need to be told it's going to be okay when you stress, even though you act like you can manage and that you'd rather be alone." She laughed.
"And I love you for that. I really do."

Chapter Fourteen

Good luck on your first day, you'll do great I know it – Haya x

Thanks H, we'll catch up soon! xx – Nay

Inayah sat at the coffee shop opposite her new job and stared at her watch whilst tapping her heels on the floor. She wondered whether she would get along with everyone and the fear of her not fitting in started to cause butterflies in her stomach. After finishing her coffee, she made her way into the building and walked over to the front desk.

"Hi, I'm here for my first day." She said clearing her throat.

"Oh yes, In...In-ayah?"

"It's Inayah.. ni like in night, and uh like umbrella."

"What? That doesn't make sense, why is it spelt like that?"

"Urm, I...I don't know, my parents-..."

"Anyways," the lady said cutting her off. "It's a busy day so if you want to take a seat I'll get Adeel to come over to you." She said raising her eyebrows.

'Snotty cow,' Inayah thought, rolling her eyes when she wasn't looking.

She sat down on the sofa, once again looking around the room at the photographs that had been framed. She thought about how one day it could be her own work framed up there.

"Inayah, welcome back, you ready for your first day?"

She looked up at Adeel and nodded with a smile.

"Great! Follow me once again, you'll get used to all this don't you worry." He said as she followed him. He started to give her a tour of the place and was speaking very quickly about everything.

"Any questions? You're pretty quiet today aren't you, is everything okay?" He asked stopping outside his office.

"Yes, sorry first day nerves I guess." She said anxiously smiling.

He took a deep breath and put his hands up so she could get the point and copy him. He smiled at her, which strangely enough calmed her down.

"Right then come in." They took a seat and started some formal paper work that she had to do before doing anything physical.

"This is contracts, your bank details because well, you obviously want to get paid." He laughed. "Just some information you need to read about the company...blah blah, yes I know it is boring but we all had to do it." He smiled again passing her yet another bundle of paper.

"Can I just say sir urm, I mean Adeel sorry. What you've achieved and done for yourself; the goals, the degree, the business it's so admirable because you've shown that it's all realistic."

"Well it wasn't easy that's the one thing people need to understand, starting up a business there's benefits but so many downfalls. There were so many days where I thought I could not achieve my dreams, days where people told me I was silly and that I couldn't do it. These are the same people that book me for their parties and weddings." He laughed. "Sorry, I'm not being smug about it all, just you know when people tell you during your whole life that you can't do it, you really feel peace when you get to say, I made it." He said shaking his head. "Sorry I've rambled on, you finished those papers?"

"Yes all done." She said passing him the pile back.

"Right then Inayah let's get shooting! Now of course I saw your portfolio and I know you have talent but I will still train you and give you the techniques we expect here at over-clicking, don't get put down if you do not establish everything straight away, it happens okay." He said. She nodded her head to show that she understood.

They made their way up the stairs and outside to the rooftop of the building. She looked nervous.

"Okay so I bring most of my newbies here because the view from here is remarkable for shooting photos. It can also show me what your strength is out of scenic, people, events all that sort of stuff. Are you okay?" He asked, noticing she did not feel at ease.

"I'm scared of heights." She said gulping, breathing in and out.
"Well that's useful isn't it?" He said laughing.
"It's...not...funny, I'm...really...not...good...with heights."
"Okay deep breath. Look at me. I'm here okay, if you fall then I'll reach over and grab you, don't worry I'm pretty strong." He laughed. "Look I just have to check your abilities, if you really struggle then I understand I'm not going to force you but as a photographer you will have to shoot at all sorts of angles and heights so maybe just give it a try and remember, I'm right here." He smiled.

"Yaseen get me down, I'm scared."
"It's not even that high!" He laughed.
"I don't care! I'll scream just help me get down I can't do this! How did you even get me to agree to this climbing?"
"Just keep looking up, don't look down."
"No I can't do it please." She said stopping.
"Inayah, we need to get across to move onto the next bit and then it's swinging down, come on look into my eyes and hold on to me."
"I am...is it over yet Yaseen? Please let's hurry."
"Well maybe if you moved your feet Inayah." He laughed.
"Okay, fine." She said, holding on to him.
"Almost done. There, we made it see! Okay hold on to me but look down."

"Are you crazy? I am not looking down I'll have a panic attack."

"Inayah I got you okay, look down, ready?"

"Oh my, we are so high, no I can't." She screamed holding on tighter.

"Yes, now look across you and at the view, take a deep breath and just pause and look." She took a deep breath.

"Wow, it's beautiful." She sniffled.

"Yeah it really is." He said smiling at her.

Inayah took a deep breath and clicked her camera towards the view.

"See that wasn't so bad right?" Adeel said.

"Yeah, can we just go down now please." She said looking glum.

"Sure." He said reassuringly as they made their way back to the inside of the building. "We'll connect them to my laptop and check them out, how does that sound?"

"Good."

"Are you okay?" He asked.

"Yeah, I'm fine thank you."

"I'm sorry I don't want you to hate this job or me because I made you do that I know I should have been more considerate but this job requires these things."

"No it's not that I'm sorry I'm just going through a lot right now and this job is actually my escape from it all." She said nervously chuckling.

"Do you want to talk about it?" He asked bringing her a drink.

"No honestly I'm not one to talk about my issues, especially not at the work place, it's okay I can be professional."

"Talk to me as a friend maybe?" He said.

"No, it's okay, I'm so sorry." She mumbled.

"Inayah don't apologise please. We all have issues come on, we're human so don't ever apologise for that because it isn't always under your control. Look, I want everyone here to feel like they can talk to me about anything and I wish for you to feel the same."

"Thank you." She smiled.

"Perhaps we should call it a day. You're off next week right for, what did you say a friend's wedding?"

"Yes that's right."

"Of course, it is wedding season! Well enjoy it and take care of yourself. Oh and Inayah, I'm only a phone call away." He said smiling walking her to the reception.

"Actually Inayah wait!" He shouted after her. She walked back towards the desk.

"Yes?"

"Well, I was just wondering if you'd like to get dinner with me tomorrow night?" He asked. She raised her eyebrows and gulped. "Not in that way don't worry I don't do dates." He laughed. "Just a professional dinner so you can get to know me as your boss but as a friend too and you can learn about the company a bit more. I actually do this with most newbies." He said.

"Oh, okay well that sounds fine." She said smiling.

"I'll text you the details." He said waving goodbye.

As he turned to walk back to his office the receptionist looked over at him.

"All the newbies yeah?" She laughed.

"Shh, our secret." He said, winking.

On her way home she started to think about Adeel and how it felt strange to associate with a man after such a long time. Perhaps deep down she felt a connection with him as he had the same passions and she admired him for reaching the goals that she dreamed of. She tried to shake that thought from her mind and tried to remind herself that it was going to be a business-related dinner, although she could not help thinking otherwise. A dark part of her reminded her that he was not, and could never be, Yaseen.

"What's he looking at?"

"He's not looking here, stop it just eat your food."

"No he's looking at you. What's his problem?"

"Yaseen calm down he's just a weirdo, just don't do anything."

"No I'm going over."

"No! Yaseen you always do this, let him look he's just pathetic you know these guys just stare, please you don't want to get into another fight."

"Fine." He scoffed.

"They can look at me as much as they like Yaseen but it's helpless when I only want and love you, so forget them."

"I know but I get jealous because you're mine, but imagine a better-looking, less tempered guy comes along and steals you away."

"That can never happen Yaseen. I've only got eyes for you."

"Promise?"

"Promise."

Chapter Fifteen

"You made it! Here take a seat." Adeel said, pulling Inayah's chair out so she could sit down. "This is one of my favourite restaurants, five-stars you know? I'm sure you'll really enjoy the food. All the celebrities come here."

"Thank you for inviting me, yeah it looks beautiful." She said as she sat down and looked around the restaurant.

"Here are your menus, sir nice to see you again." The waiter said as he bought the menus to the table. They ordered some food and waited for their drinks to arrive.

"So then why don't you tell me more about yourself, I mean I know you told me things at the interview but I'd really like to know your future plans and how you can develop them with us."

"Well, of course I'd like to grow in the company and be trained by the best, well you." She laughed. "I'm not sucking up to you, I just really admire you." She blushed.

"Thank you." He smiled. They talked throughout the night and ate their food.

"The dessert here is really good, you have to try it, all the celebrities come here." He told her once again, calling the waiter over. "Can we have the special please." He said. "I think you'll like it Inayah." Inayah looked at the table taking a deep breath from all the amazing food that she had just tasted.

"I don't know if I'll be able to eat dessert." She laughed.

"Let's take your mind off it then until it comes. So then what's life like outside of photography, what do you like to do in your spare time?"

"Well, I guess I like to spend time with my friends and family, I like movies and relaxing days." She said.

"You have so much passion when you talk about the things you love, has anyone ever told you that?" He said, causing her to blush once again.

"No, I don't think that they have." She said.

"So what's family life like?"

"It's okay I guess, it's just me and my parents I'm an only child."

"You must be very spoilt then." He laughed. "I'd say you're lucky but I do love my siblings with all my heart even if they still wind me up."

"I always wished for another sibling, but I guess I learnt how to get used to it."

"I guess when you have kids you can make sure they're not alone." He laughed.

She looked at him and bit her lip. He could tell that she felt uncomfortable.

"Sorry, touchy subject?"

"I don't really know you like that. You're my boss before anything and I don't really discuss my personal life with my friends let alone someone I work for professionally."

"I'm sorry Inayah." He mumbled awkwardly. "I just wanted to get to know you, I feel like we really have this kind of vibe, you know? You remind me of myself."

"I didn't mean to bite at you I'm sorry, I just find it hard to get close to people when I end up just losing them."

"Technically, you just opened up, do you realise that?" She looked nervous, as if she had unleashed a tornado. "Oh and Inayah, you won't lose me. I promise." He smiled.

"Oh look it's here." She said trying to change the conversation. They ate the dessert and left the restaurant. It was dark outside but the weather was humid as if it was day time. They walked over towards their cars and got ready to say their goodbyes.

"Thank you for tonight Yas-, Adeel, it was nice." She said, quickly changing her mistake hoping that he did not notice. But when he was the only thing on her mind how could his name not escape her lips.

"You're welcome and Inayah I meant what I said, so I am sorry about making things uncomfortable, I want you to be okay with me considering we're going to be working close by together a lot more." He replied.

"It's fine honestly it's okay. Thank you once again." She leaned in and hugged him.

"Inayah text me once you're home yeah?" He said.

She smiled and waved as he watched her drive away in her car.

Inayah made her way into the house and saw her mother and father were already asleep so she quietly went into her room. She felt empty inside as if her soul had somehow been grabbed and had not been returned. The feeling was mixed with guilt. She knew deep down that Adeel was a wonderful gentleman but there was a part of her that had to compare him to Yaseen. How could she not? He was everything to her and she knew that she would look for him in everyone that she met as much as she would try not to. The feelings between her and Yaseen, the way they clicked together was hard to replace and she did not know how long it would take for her to be able to find that same love, the same vibe or that comfort with anyone else. Yaseen knew her for the person that she was, he saw her through the darkness and through every battle that she faced. He knew her as well as he knew himself; from the real meaning behind her smile, or how when she twitched her nose to him it meant that she was about to cry but was holding it back and showing that she was fine.

She lay in bed and wondered how anyone else would ever be able to understand her the way that he did, but she fought with the dark thoughts and told herself that God had written something better for her and that the test of her strength and patience would soon be over.

"Is this place okay?"

"Yeah it's great Yas."

"I know it's not a five-star restaurant and my car isn't some newest edition sports car and it may break down every few weeks and I'm sorry for that, but if I could give you the world I would."

"Yaseen I don't need these fancy cars or restaurants or gifts, I just need you."

"That means a lot, because times are hard Inayah and I'm always going to remember how you stayed by my side through my struggles, how you always stayed humble about everything and never asked me for much. I love and respect you so much for that."

"You give me enough just by loving and supporting me."

"A few years from now I'll have finished my degree, I'll hopefully have a good job and I can treat you right, take you out-,"

"How about a movie, pizza and me and you sitting together? Because that alone makes the best valentines gift I could ask for."

Chapter Sixteen

"Mum has this gone tight on me?"

"Yaseen! A day before your wedding and you're trying it on now, why didn't you do it before?"

"I know but I've been busy, can you just loosen it somehow?"

"Yes I'll get someone to do it, really Yaseen you're so last minute like your lazy father."

"I'm sorry mama. I know you're also stressed."

"It's okay. Have you spoken to Aleena recently? Make sure everything is confirmed with her parents too, we need to keep on schedule okay. Did your cousins check in to the hotel?"

"Yes mum they'll be here later on."

"Good, now make sure you sleep early tonight, don't let them take you out late at night, you need to have rest; you don't want to fall asleep at your own wedding okay son?"

"Yes mama." He said joining his hands to show he was pleading her to stop with the lectures.

"Tomorrow you will be married and Aleena will be one of us." She smiled at her son. "My baby boy is all grown up." She said pinching his cheeks.

"Mum, stop it!" He smiled and went in to hug her.

"No silly drama tomorrow okay? There will be a lot of people there so we cannot embarrass ourselves." She said raising her eyebrows.

"Yes, I know." He said and made his way to his room.

Knock Knock

"Yaseen?"

"Come in."

His father walked in and took a seat on his bed, patting it to indicate he wanted him to sit.

"Yaseen, I just wanted to talk to you about tomorrow. I know your mother has probably given you her lecture but I just want to tell you that son I am very proud of you. Everything we do for you is for your benefit and I pray that this new life of yours will be full of success and happiness. Aleena is a good girl and she will bring lots of joy to your life."

"I know dad." Yaseen replied.

"I know that we have had a rocky relationship and that you should hate me for a lot of things that I have done but I love you a lot son I want you to know that I would never do anything to intentionally hurt you. As we've grown we've turned into better people together and that happens naturally with marriage too, you work together with your partner to change your ways and go through life together. It gets tough at times and you feel like you want to give up but you have such a big responsibility now and I know you'll fulfil it in the best way that you can." His father told him. He cleared his throat and smiled at his son.

"Thanks dad. I'm sorry, I love you too." He said hugging him.

Yaseen spent years of his life rebelling against his parents not understanding why they did what they did, he thought that they were cruel and strict and did not want him to live his life. It caused many arguments that ended in tears, door slams and week-long silent treatments. He matured a lot as he grew up and left his teenage tantrum days to be the man that his father tried to make him.

"Tomorrow's the big day." He whispered to himself as he laid his head on his pillow.
He closed his eyes when his phone vibrated.

Can't sleep with these nerves kicking in. Are you awake?

He opened his eyes and looked at his phone. *Aleena.*
He looked up at his ceiling and contemplated whether he should reply or not. Lost in his thoughts, he fell asleep ready for the big day tomorrow.

"Son one day you'll no longer be a seventeen-year-old, you'll have more responsibilities than you already have, going out is fine but sometimes you need to cut it down and man up."
"What is that supposed to mean? Just because I'm going out with my friends you think I'm going to do something stupid?"

"I'm just saying sometimes you youngsters go out and this world is dangerous, there is trouble everywhere."

"Dad, you don't know anything okay just leave me alone, why do you hate me so much? Why can't you let me live my life?"

"Yaseen I am protecting you!"

"Protecting me? The only trouble I'm in is the one coming from our relationship, just stay out of my life!"

"I guess he fell asleep." Aleena mumbled.

"Who?"

"Yaseen, I just texted him."

"Oh. Aleena, actually I just want to let you know that I love you and I'm really going to miss you." Noor said, sniffling.

"I'm going to miss you too Noor." She said getting out of bed to hug her.

"Listen, don't ever think you're not welcome at my new house, I'm just a phone-call away, anytime you need me, I'm here okay." Aleena said crying.

"I'm sorry for everything."

"Sisters fight Noor it happens all the time. I'm sorry too. You have to be strong at home, for mum and bhai too okay. Mum will find it really hard and you need to make her feel happy all the time okay, promise me that you will?"

"I will, I promise." She said hugging her sister tighter.

"Why do you have to take her side with everything mum?"

"She is older than you, give her some respect."

"No I hate her. You hear that Aleena? I hate you. You should have just left when dad did!"

"Do you realise what you are saying? You're angry and you're saying awful things that one day you'll regret. We are sisters not enemies Noor, we cannot fight like this, our family is already falling apart. One day I may not wake up and mum will forever take your side because she'll not have to choose between two daughters, will you be happy then?"

Chapter Seventeen

Aleena looked out of the window putting her palm against the cold glass. The sun shone through but there were grey clouds in the sky and rain was expected. She could see her family moving things into the cars that were parked outside, preparing early for the biggest day of her life. Her stomach felt uneasy as if the butterflies were real and were trying to escape. She heard a knock on the door and quickly moved away from the window.

"Come in."

"Good you are awake, here I brought you some breakfast."

"Thanks mum but I'm not very hungry."

"Aleena, you have to eat because you'll hardly get a chance to eat later, it's going to be a long day sweetheart." She told her daughter bringing the food to her desk.

"Now usually I would say eat downstairs but everyone is rushing around and I don't want you to stress at all. Once you've eaten, go take a shower and get ready and I will drop you to the hotel so the lady can start your make-up." Her mother said watching Aleena's hands shake because of the nerves. Inside she was hurting and knew that it would be an emotional day but for her daughter's sake she acted as if everything was fine.

Her phone started to vibrate with text messages and she scrolled through the 'good luck' messages to find Yaseen's name. *Nothing.*

She started to worry that he still had not replied from last night and wondered if he was okay or not. She cleared her throat and tapped his number on her phone screen.

"Hello Yaseen."

"Good morning Aleena, how you feeling?"

"I'm okay, how are you?" She lied.

"Hmm, yeah I'm okay, how's preparation?"

"Yeah it's okay just going to leave soon to get ready." She paused. "Yaseen we're going to be okay aren't we?"

"Of course Aleena, it's going to be great. I better go, got a lot to do, I'll see you later then." He said.

"Goodbye Yaseen."

She realised that the next time she would speak to him would be face-to-face and would be seconds before they accepted their marriage to one another. Her nerves were all over the place and did not know how the day would go. Aleena walked over to her drawers and took out a photo album and opened it to a certain page. She sighed when she looked at the picture of her and her father. Even though he had hurt her mother and their family, she couldn't help but miss him and wonder if he would have come to the wedding if he had known that his 'little girl' was getting married. She imagined what life would have been like if he was there and whether he would cry at her rukhsati. Her tears started to fall and she wiped them quickly realising she would be crying a lot today and knew she had to remain strong. She took a deep breath and started to get ready.

Aleena and her sister arrived at the hotel and made their way into the room that the family had booked out for Aleena to get ready in. It was a tradition for nobody to see the bride until she stepped into the hall and her house was too busy for anyone to get ready with some privacy. As she walked into the room they laid out the outfits and met the lady who was doing her hair and make-up. They started to get ready and made light conversation to keep their minds busy.

"Who would have thought weddings would be this stressful right? But don't worry you look beautiful and that was even before I touched your face." The lady laughed finishing off the final touches of make-up on Aleena's face. She pinned her scarf onto her head making sure it was still covered. Although she wore the hijab she did not want to show her hair but tried to style it in a way that most brides did.

"There, all done." The lady told them.

"Wow Aleena you look so beautiful." Noor told her.

Aleena swivelled the chair around to the mirror to have a look.

"Wow." She said, her heart starting to pace. "Thank you, you've done an amazing job." She said hugging the lady.

"You really suit the colour as well, I love the combination of blue and beige, is your other half wearing that too?"

"Yes, we planned it that way." She blushed.

"Right, well your mother messaged me to say she's waiting for you downstairs so if you want to make your way to her. Good luck with everything thank you for booking me!"

"Thank you so much!"

They made their way downstairs and many strangers passed by smiling or told Aleena that she looked beautiful.

"Aleena, my darling you look so...wow I can't describe how wonderful you look." Her mother said and her tears started. Aleena felt discomfort whenever tears left her mothers eyes, it gave her an urge to cry too.

"Mum, please don't cry, it's a happy day." Aleena smiled. She followed her mother into the car and they made their way to the venue. Her sister squeezed her hand and told her it would be okay.

"Blue will look great on us." Aleena said.

"I don't think we should wear blue."

"Why Yaseen? Don't you want me to have my dream wedding? Not many brides want to wear blue so I'll stand out you see."

"Okay Aleena, we'll wear blue, if that's what you wish."

Chapter Eighteen

After what seemed like a long journey stuck in traffic, they arrived at the venue. It was an archaic building with a large water fountain perched outside in the middle. The tyres pulled up on the stone driveway and everyone took a deep breath. Aleena's brother made his way to the tinted car with a ribbon across the front and opened the door.

"Wow Leens, you look beautiful. I hope God protects you on this special day little sis." He said smiling. She did not have her father to walk her into the hall but she had her older brother who protected her like his own from the moment she was born. As they walked towards the entrance she started to remember all the moments she shared with her brother as he held onto her arms helping her in. She recalled the times at school when she was picked on and he scared off all the kids and they stopped, or the time she was grounded and he snuck her in some ice-cream to make her feel better. It did not matter that her father was not there, her brother was the man that the family needed and she knew Yaseen had the same characteristics and mind-set to protect her like her brother did.

"Okay one more deep breath Aleena. We're about to go inside okay." Her brother whispered to her.

"Ladies and gentlemen please be seated as the bride is making her entrance." They heard a muffled announcement by the DJ from inside the hall.

"Ready?" He said as he pushed open the door as the music started.

"Yes." She whispered.

They walked inside and light shone across at them, cameras flashing and people whispering about how beautiful she looked. The venue was big and it was decorated exactly the way she had asked them. The tables were covered in white and a glass vase with blue and white flowers sat on each table. There were little gift boxes for each guest, with table wear neatly put next to them. It seemed like a very long walk to the stage but they had to walk slowly and carefully because of her heavy outfit and to stop for the photographers to capture photos every second. She could see her mother at the front of the stage sobbing as she walked in, she tried not to make eye contact because she knew she would start crying too. She looked around at the guests to take her mind off of it and looked across at her table of friends towards the front, it was a small table as most of her friends were actually family. She looked at the empty seat and noticed it was the seat Inayah was supposed to be sat in. Thoughts were running in her mind, wondering if she backed out at the last minute. Her emotions were already all over the place so she decided to just let it go, she understood when Inayah had changed her mind a few times so thought that it was fair enough. They finally reached the stage and her brother helped her sit down as the photographers came to take pictures of her with her brother, sister and mother. She looked up at the time and realised it was not long until Yaseen would be entering inside and they would be accepting their marriage together. Her heart felt heavy as if something was going to go wrong but instead she smiled as she looked up at the people around her who loved and only wanted the best for her.

Knock Knock

"Come in."

"Yaseen, wow you look great. So, why did you call me here?"

"Well I just needed help with something."

"Oh, is that all?"

"Yeah, if you don't mind."

"Sure. She looks beautiful doesn't she?"

"Yeah she does." He said looking onto the screen which showed a live stream of the hall where Aleena was seated on stage amongst the guests.

"Inayah you look beautiful too. You wore the outfit then." He smiled.

She looked down at herself in the outfit that he had sent her.

"Yeah, thank you, it was a really nice gift and the letter." She said, her voice trailing off when she realised the subject would turn emotional.

"I meant every word." He said looking into her eyes. He was about to say something else when she interrupted him.

"So what did you need help with?"

"This." He smiled, holding up a clear box.

"Inayah quick help me put this flower thing on my suit, your cousin handed it to me I've never even worn one."

"Come here silly, I'll do it."

"Thanks. Do I look nice and smart?"

"Yes, now stay still before I end up pinning it into you."

"You look beautiful too Inayah, it's your cousins wedding but all eyes will be on you." He laughed. She shook her head and smiled back.

"All done. Now you look perfect."

"Why do the men even wear these flowers in their suits they're impossible to do."

"They look nice, now get practising for your own wedding I'll be too busy to be pinning it onto you."

"Nope you're going to do it and I'll make the photographer get them cheesy couple pictures of you putting it on me, aww." He said putting his hands on her hair.

"Hey get back don't ruin my hair it took me so long to set it." She groaned. "And no way we're getting those pictures you've been watching to many romantic Bollywood movies again haven't you?" She scoffed and laughed setting her hair again.

Chapter Nineteen

She picked up the rose, and pinned it to his jacket. As she brushed down the sides, she looked at him dearly. The day he had anticipated, the day they had always talked about. He gave her a stern look, as he gulped.

"Do I look okay?" He asked.

"Of course." She smiled.

There he was in the velvet blue suit that he had always wanted to wear. Except this time, she wasn't in the matching outfit, she was not the one about to clutch on to his hand, nor was he about to place the ring on hers. A moment forever playing on their minds, from the second that their eyes had met. Fate was nothing but a distant fantasy that she could never believe in, but somehow this one person who made her feel so alive and so vibrant had this hold on her. But that hold soon turned to dust as she stood up ready to support her him on the day of his wedding. Her mouth curved with so much encouragement, yet inside she felt so lifeless.

"Thank you for coming."

"It's okay. Yaseen you need to go inside now, come on."

"I will, I just needed to say goodbye to you properly."

"Yaseen don't make this any harder than it needs to be please."

"I'm honestly sorry. I know I never said sorry to enough, even though I should have, even for the little moments. I'm sorry for every argument, fight or any moment that I caused tears to leave your eyes."

"Me too."

"Inayah, I love you so much."

"Stop it." She said, a tear starting to roll down her cheek.

"You mean the world to me and I wish I could have given you everything that you deserved but I really couldn't and I'll never forgive myself for that."

"Yaseen you're getting married today, it's going to be a fresh start for you and hopefully one for us too, so let's forget everything, we had some good memories, some good laughs, but now it's time for us to move on with our lives. I'm proud of you, you know that?" She smiled.

He looked down at the ground, his eyes starting to water.

"I'll always be praying for you."

"So will I." She told him. "Yaseen look after Aleena okay, she is an amazing girl and I think your parents made a very good choice. Her heart is so wide and she seems so humble. I know you two will support and love one another the way that we did, if not better than we did. Please try to control that temper of yours." She laughed through the tears. "Promise me, you'll do all that."

"I promise."

"Once tonight is over Yaseen you know that we can never speak again, we cannot contact one another either. If we were to bump into each other then we shall if it is written for us but for our own sake it is better to act as strangers." She choked on the last few words as if they were bullets to her chest.

There was silence as the music from the hall had stopped and the DJ cleared his throat.

"Ladies and gentlemen, the groom will now make his entrance so please do take your seats and get your cameras ready!"

"Go." She said.

"Inayah."

"Go." She said once more.

"I..." He muttered.

There was a knock on the door.

"I'm coming." He shouted towards the door as he wiped his tears. He looked up at Inayah and leaned in to hug her. She sobbed into his arms once more, recalling the thousands of times he had been there through her troubles and protected her like a shield. For the very last time he moved towards her and kissed her cheek.

"Goodbye Inayah." He said as he walked towards the door.

He turned to her once more feeling disheartened. Her tears were flowing but she smiled once more to show him it was all going to be okay and to reassure him that she herself would be fine. She could hear cheering and music playing as he walked through and his groomsmen and best man joined him from behind. She kept watching from the cameras in the room he was getting ready in as she did not feel ready to step out just yet. She needed a moment to clear her head and to get herself together before showing her face to everyone. She looked at the screen when it zoomed in on Yaseen smiling and making his way towards to the stage to join Aleena. The camera then showed Aleena trying to hide her smile as she looked up at him blushing. Inayah decided it was time to leave the room that Yaseen had called her into when she had reached the venue, she did not want to talk to him but decided it was needed for them both. She left and made her way towards her seat that she had been allocated, just as Yaseen sat down next to Aleena and placed his hand with hers. The sound of Aleena's bangles hitting against him. He smiled at Aleena and she smiled back as the photographers clicked from all the different angles. No moment was going to be missed by anyone today, every second would be captured and permanently printed for them to forever cherish. Although Inayah knew she would never see the photos after she had left she knew they would always play on her mind, the exact outfits they wore, the way they looked at one another. She knew that some day she would be out on a walk and one of the songs that played in the background of the wedding would trigger her, as if they were scars ready to be opened once more.

"Ladies and gentleman we will now perform the ceremony of the Nikaah, so if you could please keep quiet during this special moment, thank you. For those who only speak and understand English, the wedding will now begin!" The DJ announced as everyone cheered in response.

Inayah's heart started to pace as she tried to remain calm. She did not even want to look up at the stage because she could somehow feel that Yaseen's eyes were watching her and knew if she showed that she was hurting he would feel pain too. She decided to look around the room until something caught her eye.

"I'll hold you whilst you're aching, putting on a smile no matter how much I'm breaking. Because knowing that I fixed you when you felt broken, saves me more than I could ever save myself."

"That's the thing about you, you don't realise that there's this light which surrounds you and sadly you cannot see it shine, all you see is darkness veiling you. Meanwhile you stay lighting up the way for others."

Chapter Twenty

"Adeel?" She whispered to herself. Perhaps he was here as a photographer she wondered, but then realised he was in a very smart suit compared to the rest of the photographers. She gulped wondering why her fate had been written to see him at her one true love's wedding. Did Yaseen know him? He seemed to be smiling with him and Aleena, perhaps he was a friend?

"We will now begin the Nikaah ceremony." The DJ announced once again. "Please remain quiet during this part so that everyone can hear." There was mumbles by everyone who was seated as everyone started to step onto the stage, including the Imam who was going to officiate the marriage ceremony. Cameras were flashing and everyone had their phones ready to record the precious moment that was about to take place. The DJ passed a microphone to Yaseen and one to Aleena. Yaseen took the microphone and you could hear the sound of him clearing his throat. There was silence and feedback from the speakers and microphone was heard making everyone squint and hold their ears at the sound.

"Sorry." Yaseen said as he nervously laughed.

The Imam started to speak and recite to the audience, such as the meaning and importance of marriage. Inayah started to tap her fingers against the table and knew what moment was coming next. She looked around as her surroundings started to blur, she tried to shake her head to keep her vision and thoughts clear but felt uneasy.

"Aleena Nazir do you accept this marriage to Yaseen Ali?"

"Qubool hai." She answered, her voice shaking as soon as she had opened her lips.

There were some celebrating noises from the audience but they were hushed by the Imam who needed silence during the process.

"Yaseen Ali, do you accept this marriage to Aleena Nazir?"

There was a moment of silence as he looked around the room. All eyes were on him, this exact moment that he had played in his head, except there was supposed to be somebody else next to him. He looked up at the table and saw Inayah, the one woman he cherished and loved and had to throw away a whole life with. He thought about the plans that they had, the memories they made, the future talk, the baby names they would always laugh about. He thought about the moments where he was hurting and she was his saviour healing him, giving him a reason to keep going.

"Yaseen Ali, do you accept this marriage to Aleena Nazir?" The Imam repeated. There were murmurs from the guests as they started to whisper about why Yaseen had not replied. Inayah looked up at Yaseen and slowly nodded, smiling, indicating that it was okay. He took a deep breath. Aleena looked over at him from the corner of her eye, trying not to move.

"Qubool hai." He said.

"Both parties have accepted the marriage, Mubarak ho, congratulations to all of you." Everyone started to cheer and the music started. Confetti was being thrown from all angles of the stage and everyone was meeting each other giving their congratulations to one another. Yaseen smiled at Aleena and took her hand once more. He took the small box from his pocket and pulled out the lavish ring and placed it onto her shaking finger. Her mother passed her the ring for Yaseen and she placed it onto his finger too. Once again everyone cheered and there were flashes from all the cameras.

One by one families started to go up and take photos with the newlywed couple, blocking the view of them to the ones who remained seated. Inayah decided to freshen up as the last few moments had drained her. As she was walking to the bathroom someone stopped her in her tracks.

"Inayah, what a pleasant surprise."

"Adeel." She smiled. "I thought I saw you but I wasn't too sure if you were working or not." She told him.

"Actually I'm here to attend the wedding, I didn't know that this was the wedding you were talking about." He laughed.

"Are you from the groom's side or brides?"

"I'm Aleena's brother." He said smiling. He started to question her about how she knew Aleena or whether she was here as Yaseen's guest, but her mind was focused on another thing. Her new boss who suddenly had shown interest in her, taken her out for dinner and tried to be there for her was related to Aleena. Was it all planned from the start? She did not know what to think, her trust issues were all over the place. Did he know about her and Yaseen's past and realise why she was so upset during work?

"Her brother?" She asked confused.

"Yes her brother. Can't you tell by our looks? Everyone says she looks like me." He told her. "I don't know who should be more insulted." He whispered sarcastically and laughed. "I walked her in didn't you see?"

"No I missed the entrance, I was running late." She lied, truthfully she was in the room but her view was only of the back of Aleena and Adeel's heads.

"So are you a friend of hers or my new brother-in-law?" The words rolling off his tongue so easily.

"Both."

"Oh wow really that's nice. Small world right, that we would meet like this again, maybe it's for a reason." He winked and smirked.

"Adeel!" A voice shouted.

"Anyways, Inayah I better go, I'll see you around." He said patting his hand on her shoulder as he left.

Inayah was puzzled once more. Would she be able to stay at the job knowing that she would not have the fresh start that she wanted? She would be giving up one of her biggest dreams because of her problems that never seemed to leave her. Inayah thought about how one day she could be in the office and Yaseen and Aleena could come to visit Adeel and she would have to see them too. It was tormenting her just thinking about those moments.

"Ladies and Gentlemen, the newlywed couple will now cut the cake." The DJ announced. She hurried to the bathroom and freshened up like she was supposed to and quickly sat in her chair. Yaseen took Aleena's hand and walked towards the three-tiered cake which was placed on a singular table ready for them to cut. The music started playing and people started to countdown till they cut the cake.

"3...2...1!" They all cheered as they cut the cake hand in hand smiling at one another. Aleena took some of the cake and fed her husband. Yaseen then prepared to do the same and picked up some cake and smeared it on her face causing her eyes to widen. He grabbed a napkin and wiped her face and gave her a side hug out of sympathy, but could not hold back his laughter. Everyone joined in laughing and carried on celebrating the precious moment. Inayah sat and watched Yaseen; his habits, his movement, his expressions – nothing about him had changed.

"Happy birthday!"
"Thank you."
"Make a wish and blow the candles."
"Okay done."
"Okay feed me cake then."
"Fine. Ow you bit me Yas!"
"Sorry." He laughed. "Okay my turn open wide."
"Ahh."
"Wider."
"Ahh...Yaseen!"
"Did you really think that I wouldn't do it."
"It's all over my face, you ruined my make-up, you're so lucky it's not in my hair."
"You know you're laughing don't lie." He laughed.
She laughed and grabbed the remaining cake from her hand and threw it onto his face to call it even.

Chapter Twenty-One

"Congratulations guys." Inayah said looking at the couple. She had joined them on stage to hand them their gifts and give them her best wishes. "You both look amazing together." She said looking back and forth at them both. "Yaseen you better look after her okay." Inayah laughed, hiding the pain. Aleena grinned.

"Thank you so much for coming." She whispered as she hugged her.

"Photo time guys!" The photographer shouted. Everyone stood together and smiled for the camera. If only the camera could capture the emotions that they really felt instead of the smiles that they showed.

"Wait." They heard from the crowd. "Me too." Adeel said stepping up onto the stage.

He stood next to Inayah nudging her lovingly as the photographer began to take the picture. She cleared her throat and shook her head at him. He laughed and jokingly put his fist against her shoulder. Inayah looked up and noticed Yaseen was watching the pair of them, his eyes looked red as if steam was ready to come out of his nose. Inayah grabbed Adeel's arm and walked towards the exit with him, not worrying about what others would say. She noticed that Yaseen was watching them and perhaps wondering how they knew each other.

"What are you doing Inayah?" Adeel questioned.

"I have to speak to you." She gulped.

People walked past giving them looks, wondering what was going on between the two of them.

"This, whatever you're doing has to stop okay."

"Inayah it's just a joke what's gotten into you?"

"Adeel I'm Yaseen's ex-girlfriend." She blurted out. "We were in love for many years, he left me when his arrangement with Aleena came around, then we stopped speaking I accepted it because I understood. Aleena and me we started speaking, it's a long story but I decided I would come to the wedding and then that's it, I was going to walk out of their lives and have my own fresh start and then you came along." She said, catching her breath after she let it all out without a gasp of air.

He was silent, for once not knowing what to say.

"I see."

"You're great, amazing in fact but I just got out of this relationship and this is all really hard for me. Yaseen will be amazing to Aleena I promise you that he really will, it's completely over for us but I just need to walk away and let them live on. Do you see where I'm going with this?"

"You're quitting?"

"Yes."

"You have astounding skills as a photographer Inayah, why throw it all away?"

"It's hard I know but for their sake I have to cut off all relations, I know it was not my place to tell you all this but you yourself said to me once that I could come to you about anything."

"I know. Inayah I started to really like you, like I said the day that we first met, you remind me of myself. I'm not going to judge you or think badly of Yaseen I know he'll love and cherish my sister. I'll tell you what I've got a couple of links to some of the best photography firms and businesses, how about I transfer you to one of them instead?"

"You would really do that for me?" She said, her eyes widening.

"Of course. You're talented and your heart is pure. For you to give up something you're so passionate about for two people who I'm pretty sure you probably should be disliking, it just shows what kind of person you are."

"Thank you so much Adeel." She said hugging him tightly.

"I mean it though, I'm here if you ever need me. Who knows perhaps someday I'll book you for my own wedding when you're running your own top firm." He smirked.

"Perhaps." She laughed shaking his hand. "Thank you once more." She said smiling, as she walked away from him. For the first time that day she felt content as if things could be going right for her.

Throughout the night there was delicious food served, as well as desserts. The music was constantly playing and people were singing and dancing with one another. Many people who had recognised her came up and asked her how she was doing but she smiled at each person and told them that she was fine. Everyone seemed cheerful and delighted to be there and Inayah knew that she had made the right choice coming.

"Ladies and gentlemen our wonderful guests, I'd like to thank you all for coming and once again, congratulations to my son and new daughter-in-law, welcome to the family Aleena." Yaseen's father said into the microphone. "May you both have a blessed life and future with one another and continue to help each other through every moment of happiness and sadness. The rukhsati will begin shortly so please do clear the pathway for everyone to leave. Thank you." He said indicating to the guests that Aleena would be leaving with Yaseen soon.
The rukhsati was the most emotional part of the night where the bride would leave with the groom's family, it was where her own family would say goodbye to her. Inside Inayah thought that it was not just a rukhsati for Aleena but one for her too, she was parting from Yaseen for the very last time.

"I know we've been friends for a few months now but honestly I think I really like you and we're only eleven years old but Inayah you make me smile and laugh and I don't know why but I feel like I'm flying when I'm with you. Will you be mine?"

"I feel the same way with you but I don't want to ruin our friendship and we're kids I mean I don't want this to be one of those one-month little relationships okay."

"Then let's promise that even when we're together we'll also be friends and our friendship will always come first because I don't want to lose you either. One month, you and I lady, we're going to make it to the end!"

"Deal! You really think so?"

"Call me a fool but I've thought so from the moment that I looked your way."

Chapter Twenty-Two

Suddenly the music had turned off and the crowd of guests closed in together. Aleena's mother and sister came next to her and gave her a big hug and every other guest slowly followed in saying farewell to the newlyweds. Each person had tears in their eyes out of happiness, yet were sad that they were saying goodbye. Aleena was starting a new life and when a woman of their culture got married it was as if she was leaving the family to go to her new family; the grooms side. Yaseen had a stern face as he held Aleena's hand and walked her through the hall towards the car that was going to drive them home. They were saying goodbye to him as well as Aleena and giving him the 'take care of her or else' look. The crowd of guests followed them outside one by one as they made their way through the door outside. Aleena's mother once more gave her a hug, eyes blood-shot red from the tears, telling her she loved her and she was always going to be there for, which caused Aleena to cry more as she let go of her mother's hand.

Inayah walked out behind the people, knowing that this moment would not be easy for her but she knew that she had to be there. She watched as everyone was sobbing very loudly as if they were mourning the loss of someone. She looked up at Adeel and saw him holding back his tears and acting strong for his mother and sister, telling them that it would be okay and that Aleena would be fine.

He walked over to his little sister, the one he watched grow up, he held on to her hand and said his goodbye. Letting go of her fingers was painful, remembering the moments that she would hold on to his hands and hide behind him when their father and mother would argue and how he would use his hands to wipe her tears when she cried. He once more wiped those tears for the very last time and kissed her cheek goodbye as he opened the car door. He looked around the crowd of guests who were shoving around to say goodbye and met with Inayah's eyes. He nodded to indicate to her to come forward as they were leaving. She shook her head and gave him a sympathetic smile. He nodded once more. She knew he was right, she had to go forward before she regretted it.

She treaded softly towards the car where Aleena was getting ready to sit inside and came in front of her. Aleena looked up at her, with a remorseful face.

"Inayah." She cried, hugging the woman who just a few months ago she had never met but only imagined what she was like in the stories told by her new husband. The woman she always envied because although she was the one walking away with the man she cherished, she knew she would never forget the light she brought to Inayah's life.

"Good luck with everything, congratulations once again." Inayah said, barely being able to speak through her tears, hugging her for the last time. She looked up at Yaseen who was trying to firmly look away but could not help but look at her with sorrow in his eyes. She turned to him and hugged him once more and whispered into his ear for the very last time.

"I love you and I'm proud of you. I wish you the best, please look after her and yourself Yaseen. Goodbye" She cried. The guests were all around them but in the few seconds that they had to say goodbye, it was as if the world had frozen for just one moment.

"Goodbye Inayah." He said as tears started to form in his heavy eyes. He blinked quickly and sat inside the car before anybody noticed. Aleena joined him from the other side and sat down too, waving from the open window. The car was ready to leave and the men of her family pushed the car out of tradition of saying farewell for the last time. Soon after the rest of Yaseen's family followed the cars and made their way home. The remaining families from Aleena's side started to prepare to leave too, still upset over their loved one leaving.

Inayah watched the car drive away, for the very last time they were parting and this time he was not alone. She started to walk towards her own car and knew she felt empty inside but there was a glimmer of ease. Someone could watch her and see her as a normal person who turned up to the wedding, not realising all those moments she forced herself not to attend. They would not know about how much she planned to be sitting on the stage next to Yaseen's side, both wearing the matching outfits, having their first dance to the song he would always sing to her at 3am when he called her up because he missed her.

Although her heart was aching, she knew that every single moment between her and Yaseen; from the second that they laid eyes on one another and said hello, to their very last goodbye, had been written for them. Inayah knew that although the love of her life had walked away from her, the journey to that point was unforgettable. They supported and cared for one another and moulded each other into the people that they were today. Every memory that they had reminded her exactly how he helped to turn her into the person that she was today. He gave her a reason to keep going and get out of bed each morning, he told her to follow her dreams and gave her the confidence to achieve her goals. He was a part of her soul and always would remain in her heart, whether it was his wise words constantly lingering and reminding her to keep going, or just giving her a reason to smile when remembering everything. He was a treasure she would forever value. She knew deep down that the pain was all worth it, like she had always been told by the teachings of Islam itself, 'verily with hardship, there comes ease.'

To my Yaseen,

I hope that she keeps you happy;
the way that I prayed I could.
I wonder if she'll accept you,
after you tell her all that you've been through.
I hope that she understands you,
and you let her in sooner than you let me in.
Because she may not have the patience to put up with the
insecurities like I did.
Darling I hope you erased the memories,
even though it took me a while.
I wonder if you'll have the grand wedding that you desired.
I hope you get your future dreams, baby names and all.
I wonder if you'll teach them, the things we discussed before.
I hope they all get used to, those sarcastic jokes you make.
As well as learn to put up with, that annoying 'told you so'
look you get on your face.
I hope that your prayers are answered,
and I wish you the best in life.
But most of all I hope you've found the one;
who will stay by your side.

From your Inayah.

Allhamdullilah.

17719168R00068

Printed in Great Britain
by Amazon